MOJANG

MINECRAFT™

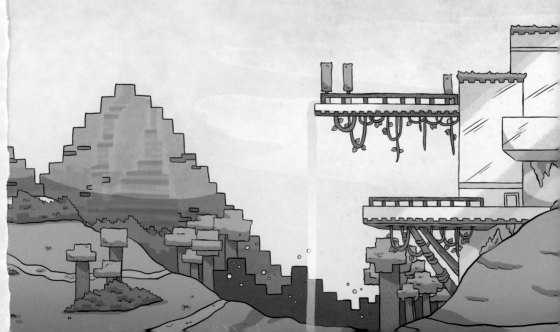

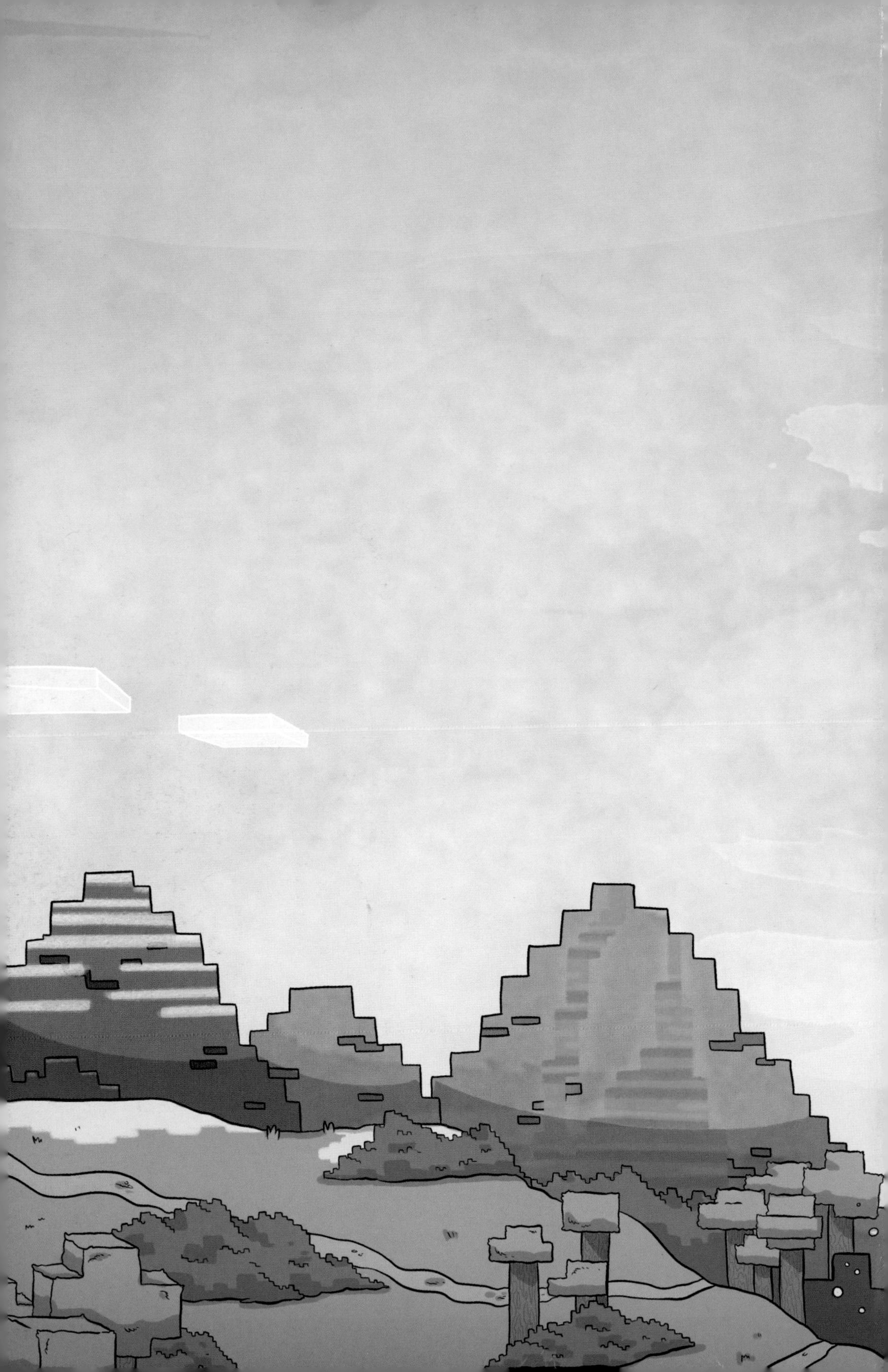

MOJANG

MINECRAFT™

WRITTEN BY
SFÉ R. MONSTER

ART AND COVER BY
SARAH GRALEY

COLOR ASSISTANCE BY
STEF PURENINS

LETTERED BY
JOHN J. HILL

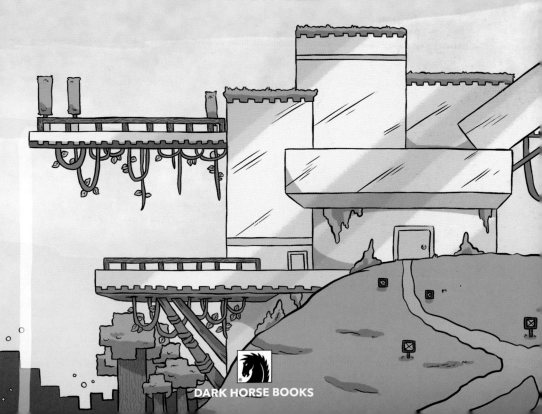

DARK HORSE BOOKS

PRESIDENT & PUBLISHER
MIKE RICHARDSON

EDITOR
SHANTEL LaROCQUE

ASSISTANT EDITOR
BRETT ISRAEL

DESIGNER
KEITH WOOD

DIGITAL ART TECHNICIAN
JOSIE CHRISTENSEN

SPECIAL THANKS TO
**JENNIFER HAMMERVALD,
ALEX WILTSHIRE,** AND
RACHEL ROBERTS.

Published by Dark Horse Books
A division of Dark Horse Comics LLC
10956 SE Main Street
Milwaukie, OR 97222

MINECRAFT.NET
DARKHORSE.COM

To find a comics shop in your area, visit ComicShopLocator.com.

Scholastic edition: December 2019
ISBN 978-1-50671-723-4

10 9 8 7 6 5 4 3 2 1

Printed in China

NEIL HANKERSON
Executive Vice President

TOM WEDDLE
Chief Financial Officer

RANDY STRADLEY
Vice President of Publishing

NICK McWHORTER
Chief Business Development Officer

DALE LaFOUNTAIN
Chief Information Officer

MATT PARKINSON
Vice President of Marketing

CARA NIECE
Vice President of Production and Scheduling

MARK BERNARDI
Vice President of Book Trade and Digital Sales

KEN LIZZI
General Counsel

DAVE MARSHALL
Editor in Chief

DAVEY ESTRADA
Editorial Director

CHRIS WARNER
Senior Books Editor

CARY GRAZZINI
Director of Specialty Projects

LIA RIBACCHI
Art Director

VANESSA TODD-HOLMES
Director of Print Purchasing

MATT DRYER
Director of Digital Art and Prepress

MICHAEL GOMBOS
Senior Director of Licensed Publications

KARI YADRO
Director of Custom Programs

KARI TORSON
Director of International Licensing

SEAN BRICE
Director of Trade Sales

Library of Congress Cataloging-in-Publication Data

Names: Monster, Sfe R., writer. | Graley, Sarah, illustrator. | Hill, John
   J. (Letterer), letterer.
Title: Minecraft / written by Sfe R. Monster ; illustrated by Sarah Graley ;
   lettered by John J. Hill.
Description: First edition. | Milwaukie, OR : Dark Horse Books, 2019. |
   Series: [Minecraft ; volume 1]
Identifiers: LCCN 2019000776 | ISBN 9781506708348 (paperback)
Subjects: LCSH: Graphic novels. | BISAC: JUVENILE FICTION / Comics & Graphic
   Novels / Media Tie-In.
Classification: LCC PZ7.7.M646 Min 2019 | DDC 741.5/973--dc23
LC record available at https://lccn.loc.gov/2019000776

MINECRAFT™

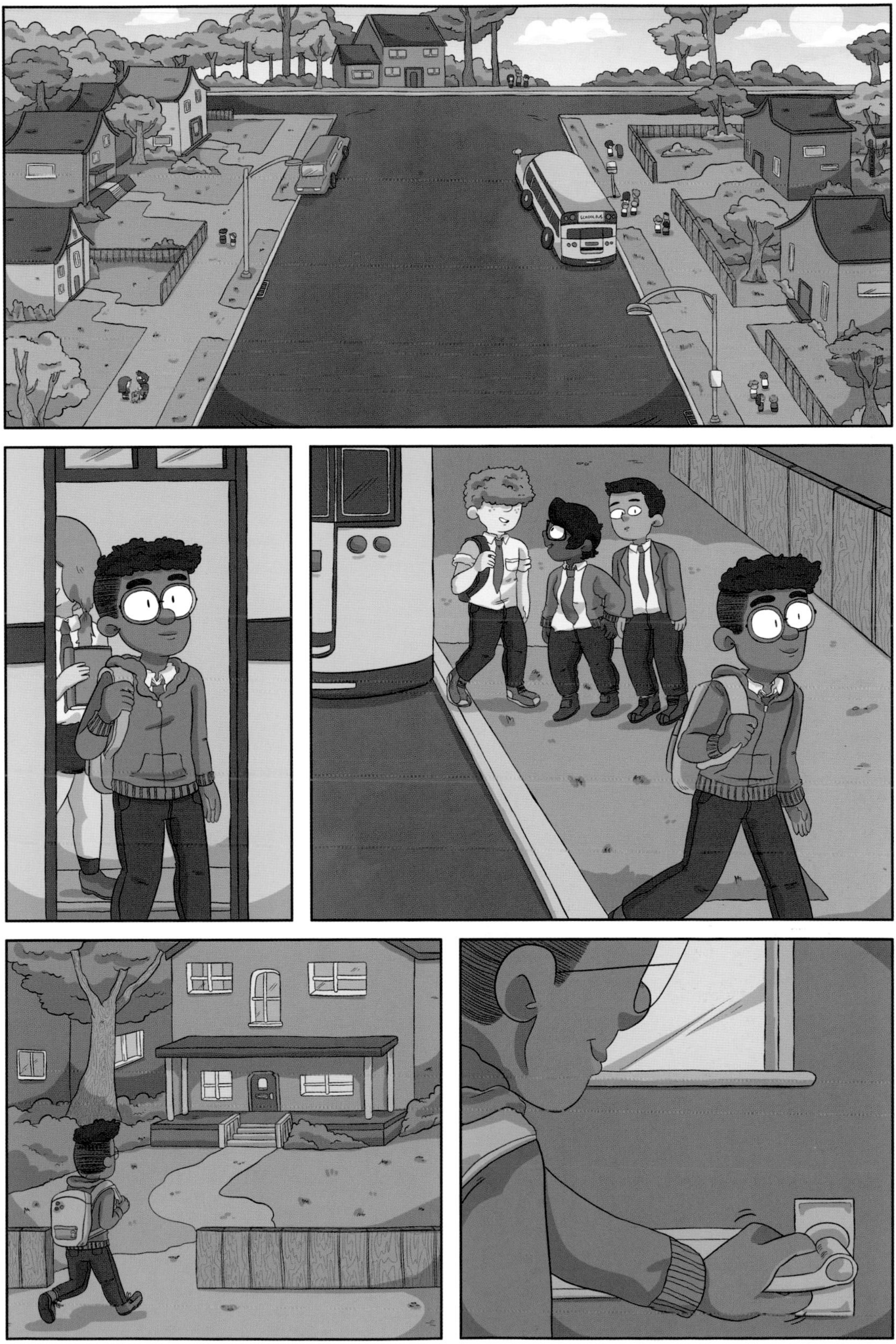

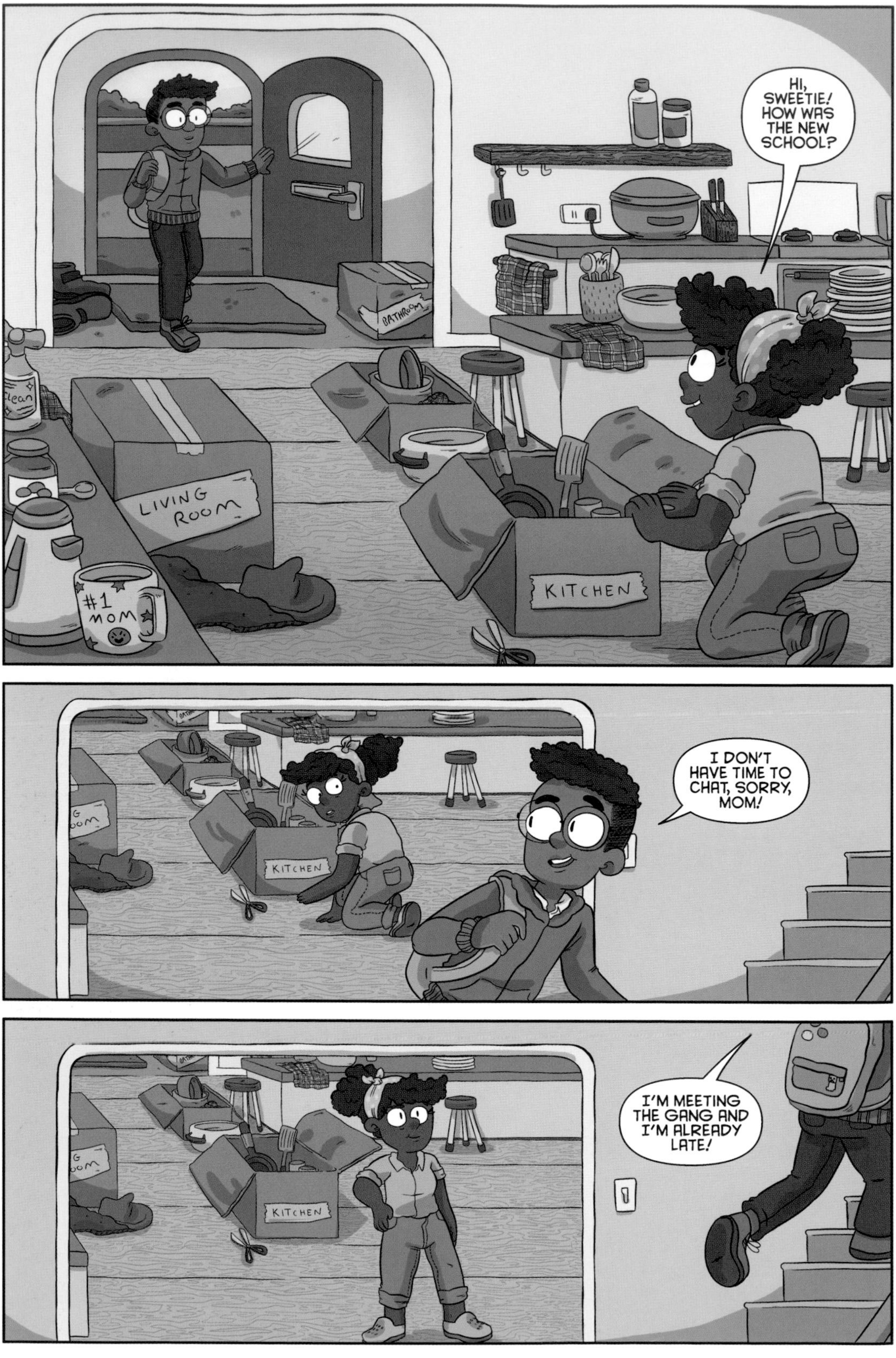
HI, SWEETIE! HOW WAS THE NEW SCHOOL?
LIVING ROOM
BATHROOM
KITCHEN
Clean
#1 MOM
I DON'T HAVE TIME TO CHAT, SORRY, MOM!
KITCHEN
I'M MEETING THE GANG AND I'M ALREADY LATE!
KITCHEN

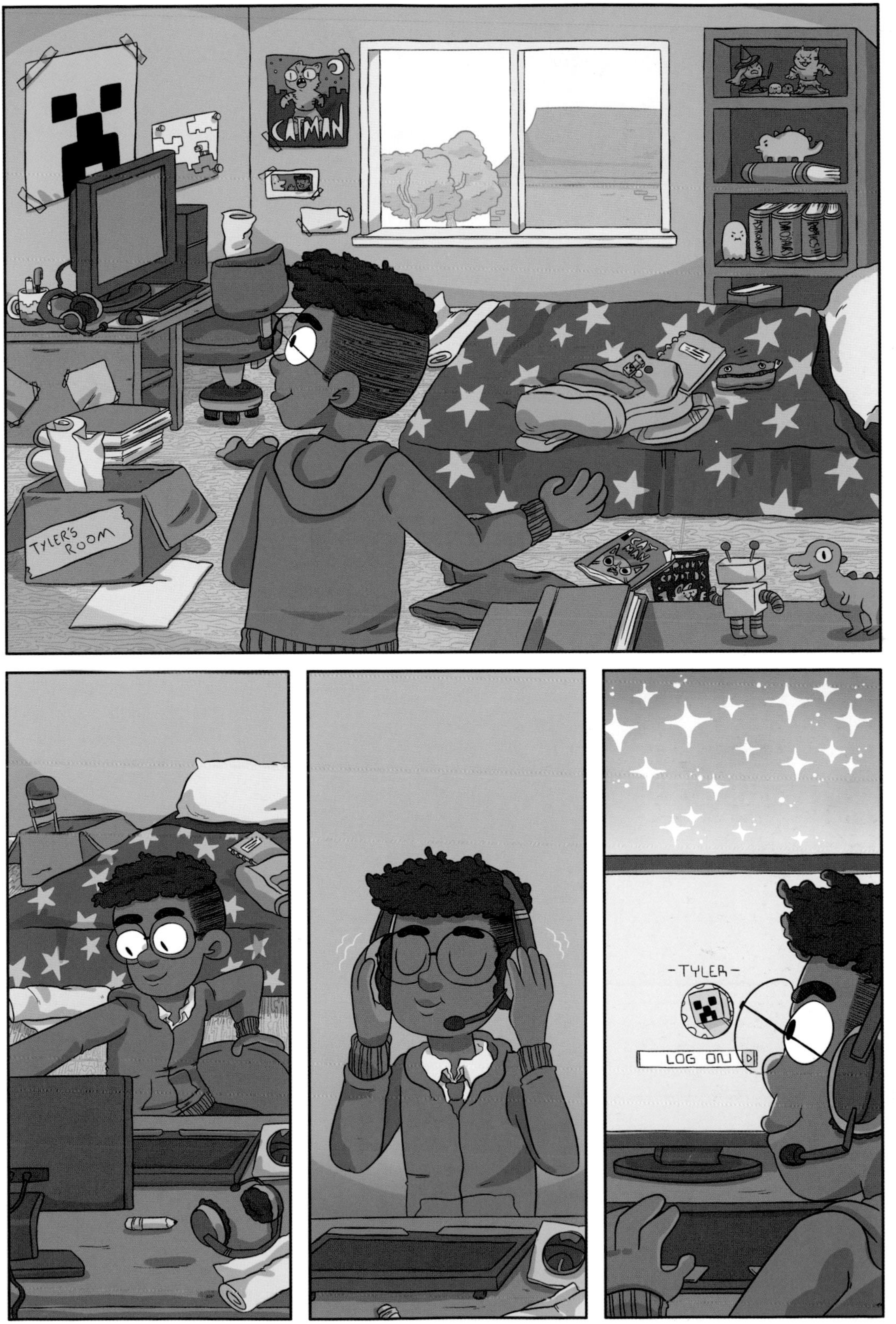
CATMAN
TYLER'S ROOM
CAT MAN
-TYLER-
LOG ON

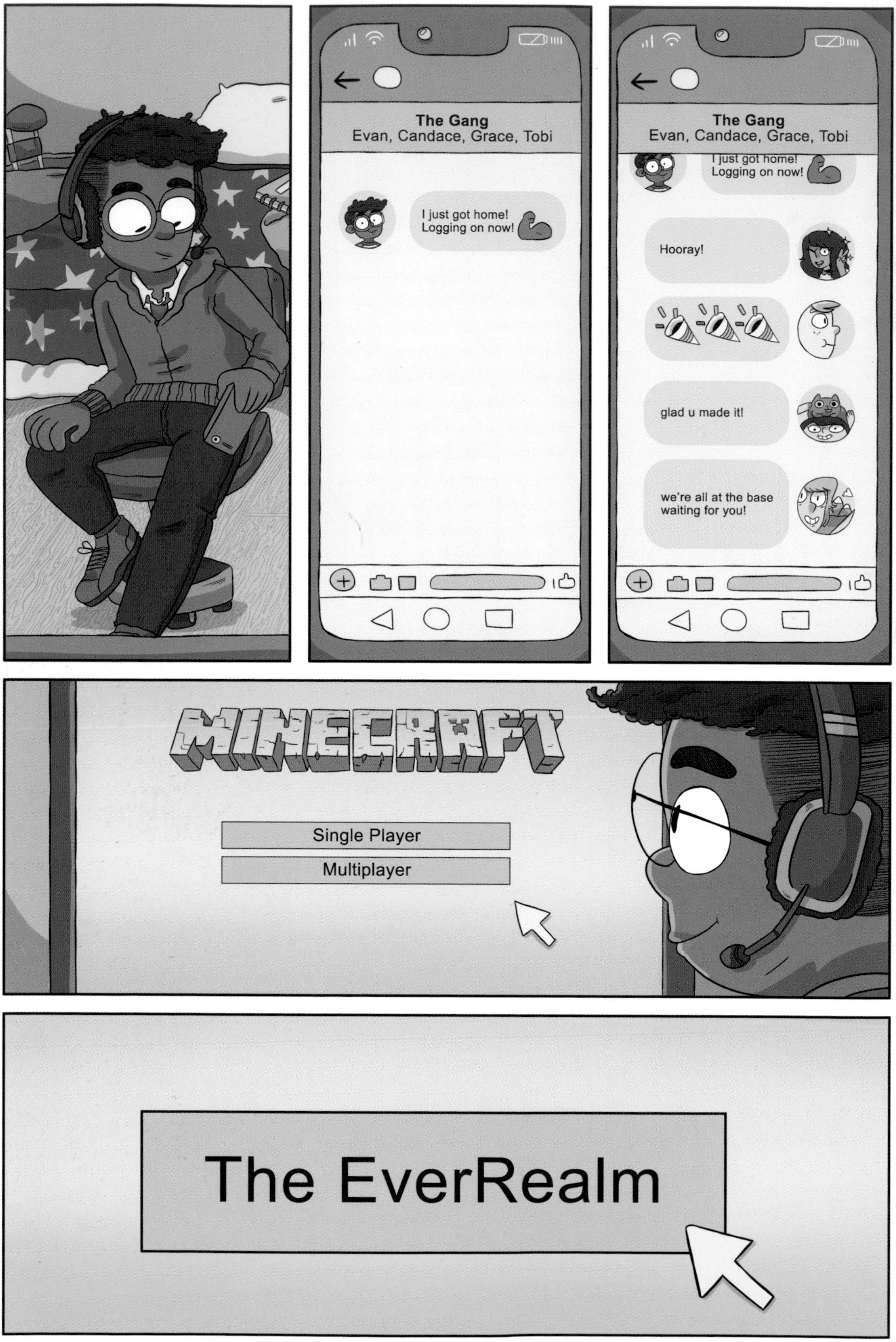
The Gang
Evan, Candace, Grace, Tobi
I just got home! Logging on now!
The Gang
Evan, Candace, Grace, Tobi
I just got home! Logging on now!
Hooray!
glad u made it!
we're all at the base waiting for you!
MINECRAFT
Single Player
Multiplayer
The EverRealm

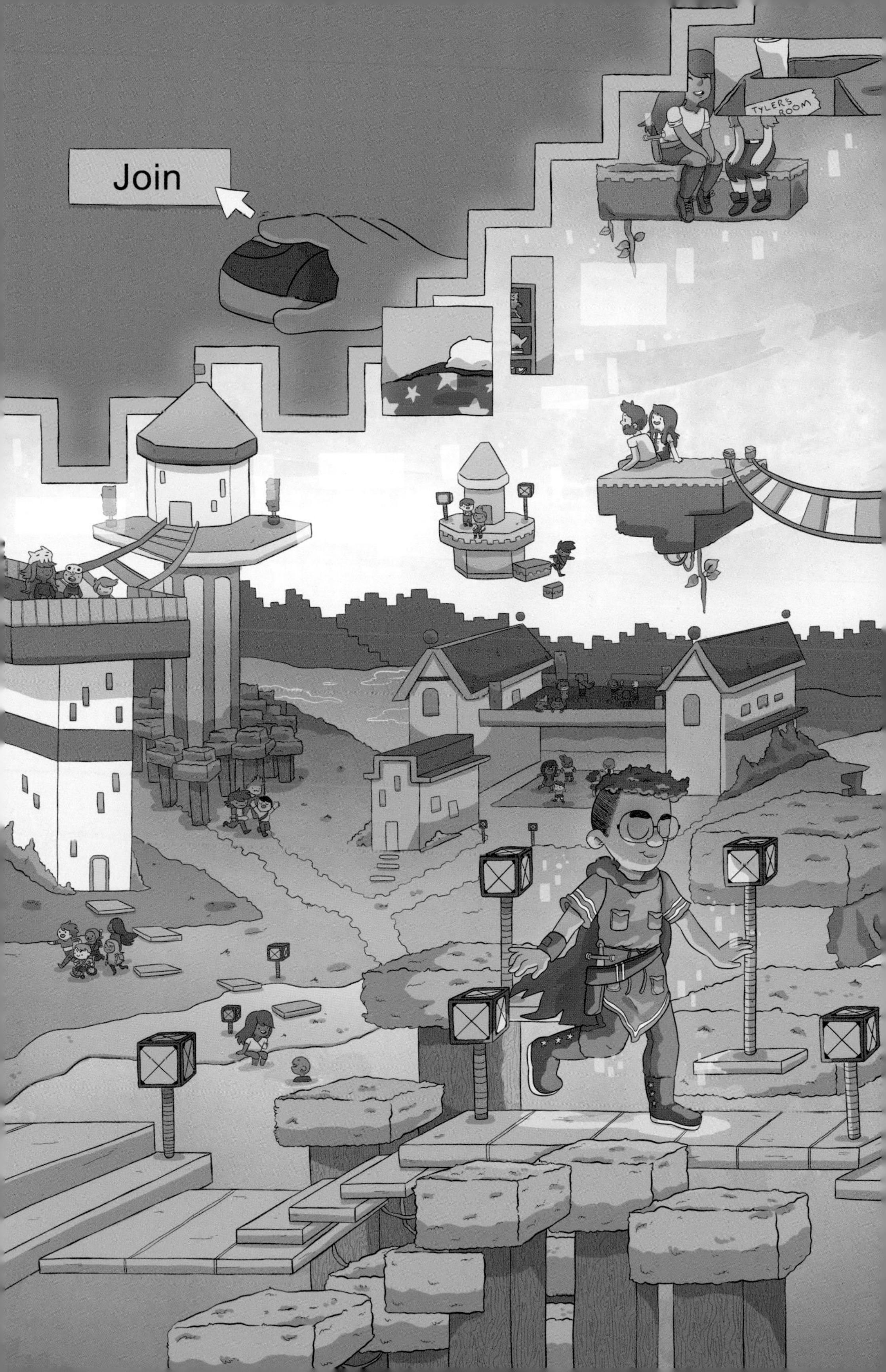
Join
TYLER'S ROOM

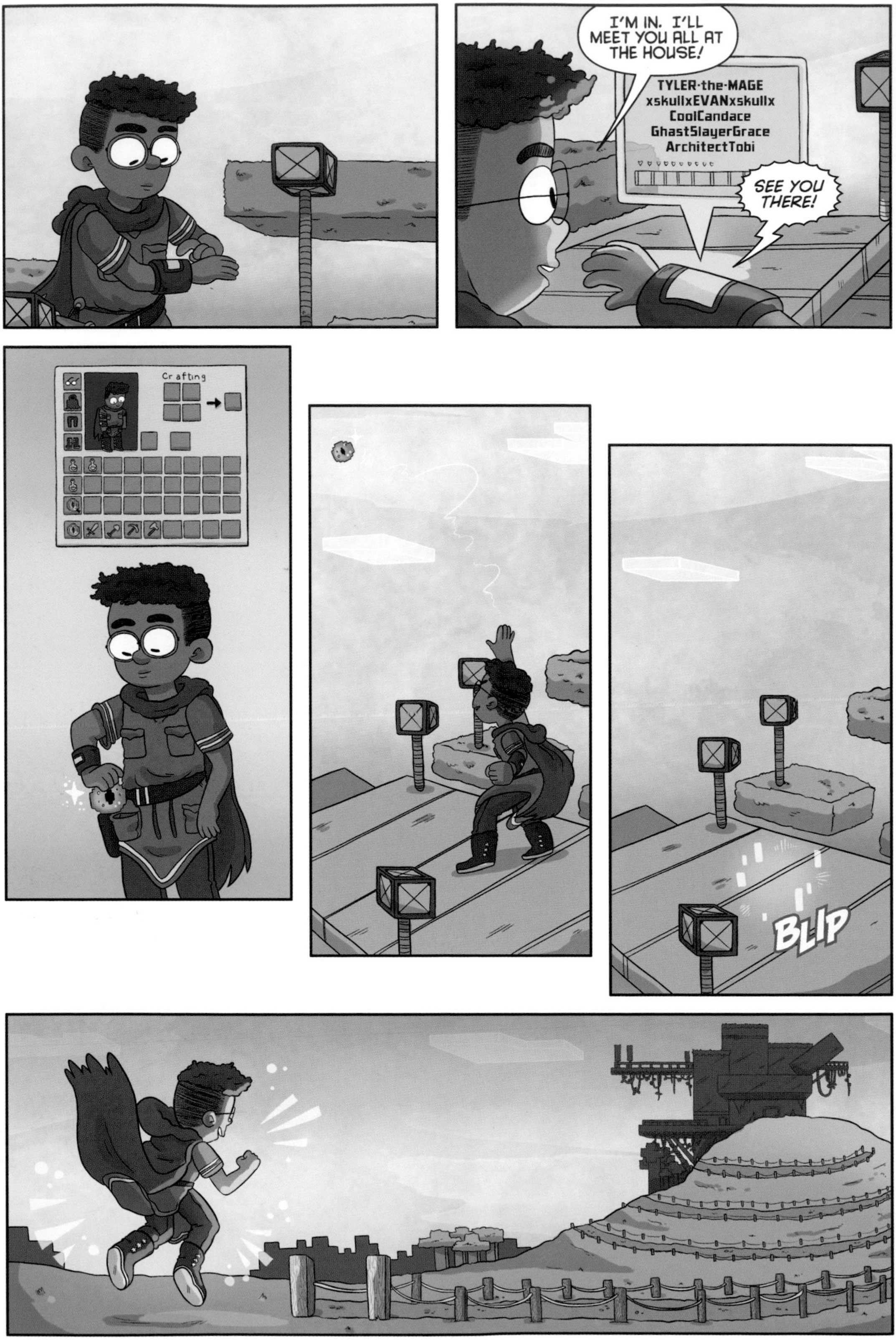
I'M IN. I'LL MEET YOU ALL AT THE HOUSE!
TYLER-the-MAGE
xskullxEVANxskullx
CoolCandace
GhastSlayerGrace
ArchitectTobi
SEE YOU THERE!
Crafting
BLIP

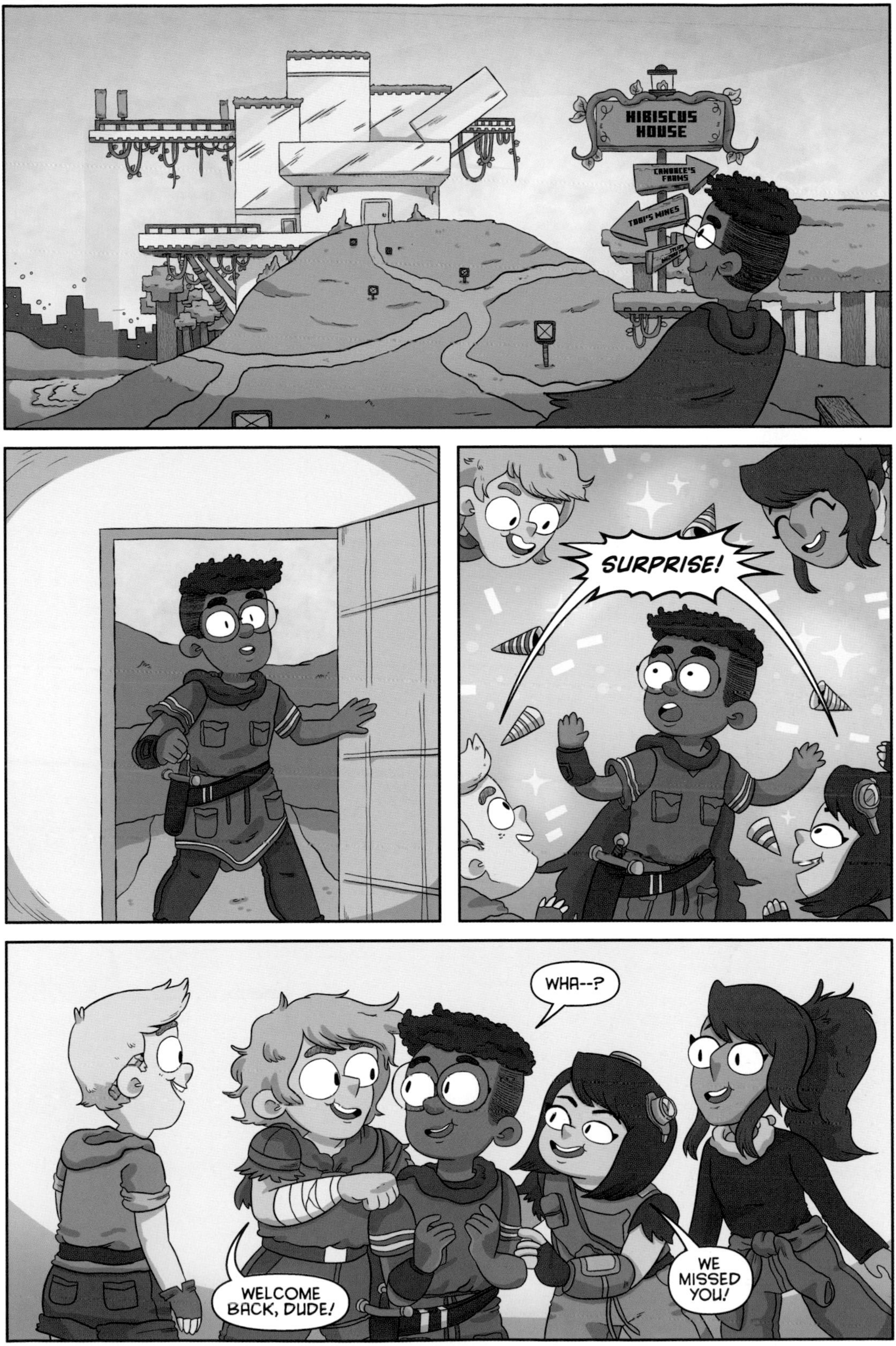

HIBISCUS HOUSE
CANDACE'S FARMS
TOBI'S MINES
SURPRISE!
WHA--?
WELCOME BACK, DUDE!
WE MISSED YOU!

WHAT'S ALL THIS FOR?

WE WANTED TO CELEBRATE YOUR RETURN AFTER YOUR BIG CROSS-COUNTRY MOVE!

IT'S THE FIRST TIME WE'VE ALL BEEN ABLE TO PLAY TOGETHER SINCE YOU LEFT! WE HAD TO MAKE IT SPECIAL, TYLER.

LOOK, WE MADE YOU A CAKE AND EVERYTHING!

AWW, YOU GUYS!

C'MON, TELL US EVERYTHING! HOW'S THE MOVING GOING!?

HOW'S YOUR NEW SCHOOL?

ANY COOL NEW FRIENDS??

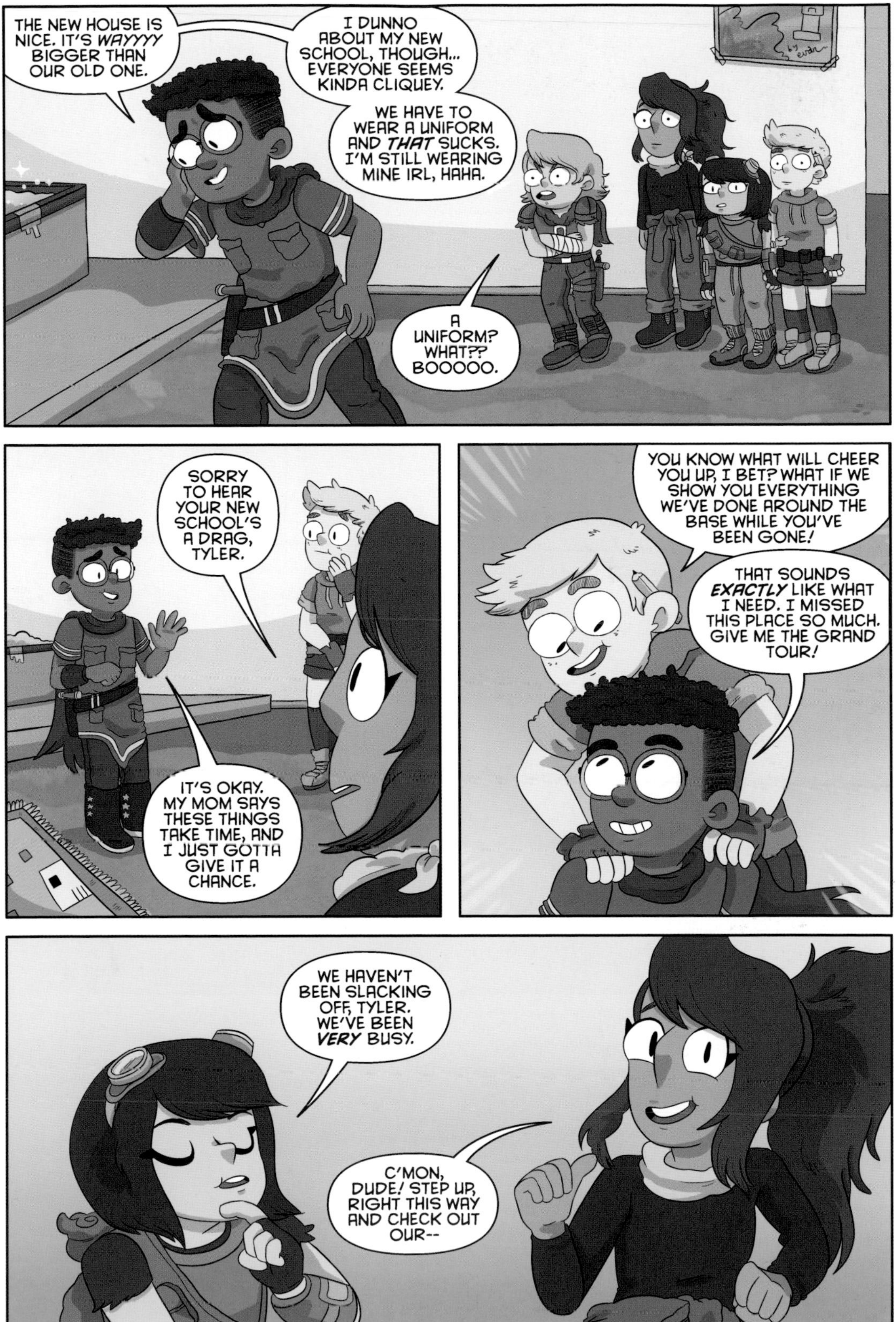
THE NEW HOUSE IS NICE. IT'S WAYYYY BIGGER THAN OUR OLD ONE.
I DUNNO ABOUT MY NEW SCHOOL, THOUGH... EVERYONE SEEMS KINDA CLIQUEY.
WE HAVE TO WEAR A UNIFORM AND THAT SUCKS. I'M STILL WEARING MINE IRL, HAHA.
A UNIFORM? WHAT?? BOOOOO.
SORRY TO HEAR YOUR NEW SCHOOL'S A DRAG, TYLER.
IT'S OKAY. MY MOM SAYS THESE THINGS TAKE TIME, AND I JUST GOTTA GIVE IT A CHANCE.
YOU KNOW WHAT WILL CHEER YOU UP, I BET? WHAT IF WE SHOW YOU EVERYTHING WE'VE DONE AROUND THE BASE WHILE YOU'VE BEEN GONE!
THAT SOUNDS EXACTLY LIKE WHAT I NEED. I MISSED THIS PLACE SO MUCH. GIVE ME THE GRAND TOUR!
WE HAVEN'T BEEN SLACKING OFF, TYLER. WE'VE BEEN VERY BUSY.
C'MON, DUDE! STEP UP, RIGHT THIS WAY AND CHECK OUT OUR--

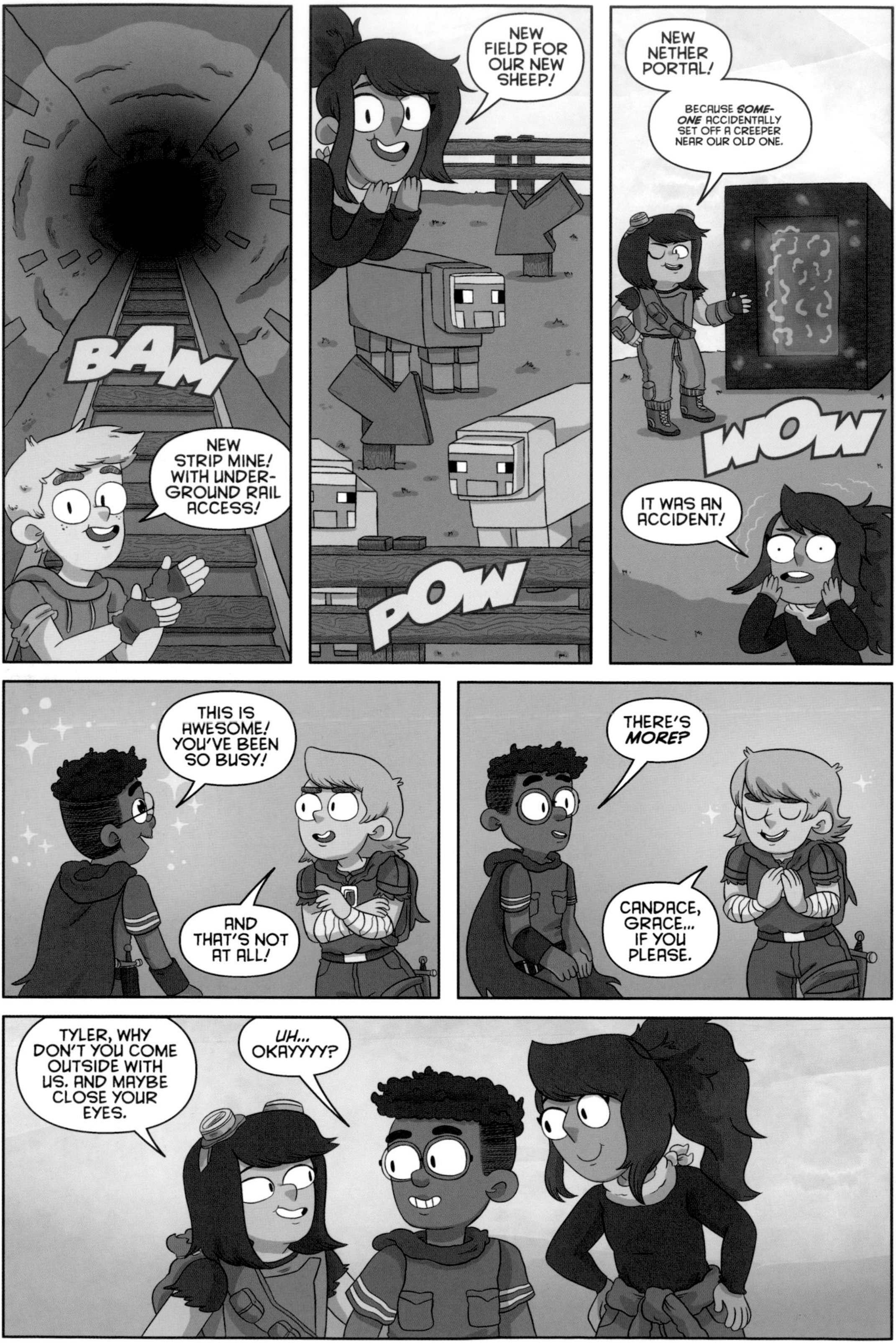
BAM
NEW STRIP MINE! WITH UNDER-GROUND RAIL ACCESS!
NEW FIELD FOR OUR NEW SHEEP!
POW
NEW NETHER PORTAL!
BECAUSE SOME-ONE ACCIDENTALLY SET OFF A CREEPER NEAR OUR OLD ONE.
WOW
IT WAS AN ACCIDENT!
THIS IS AWESOME! YOU'VE BEEN SO BUSY!
AND THAT'S NOT AT ALL!
THERE'S MORE?
CANDACE, GRACE... IF YOU PLEASE.
TYLER, WHY DON'T YOU COME OUTSIDE WITH US. AND MAYBE CLOSE YOUR EYES.
UH... OKAYYYY?

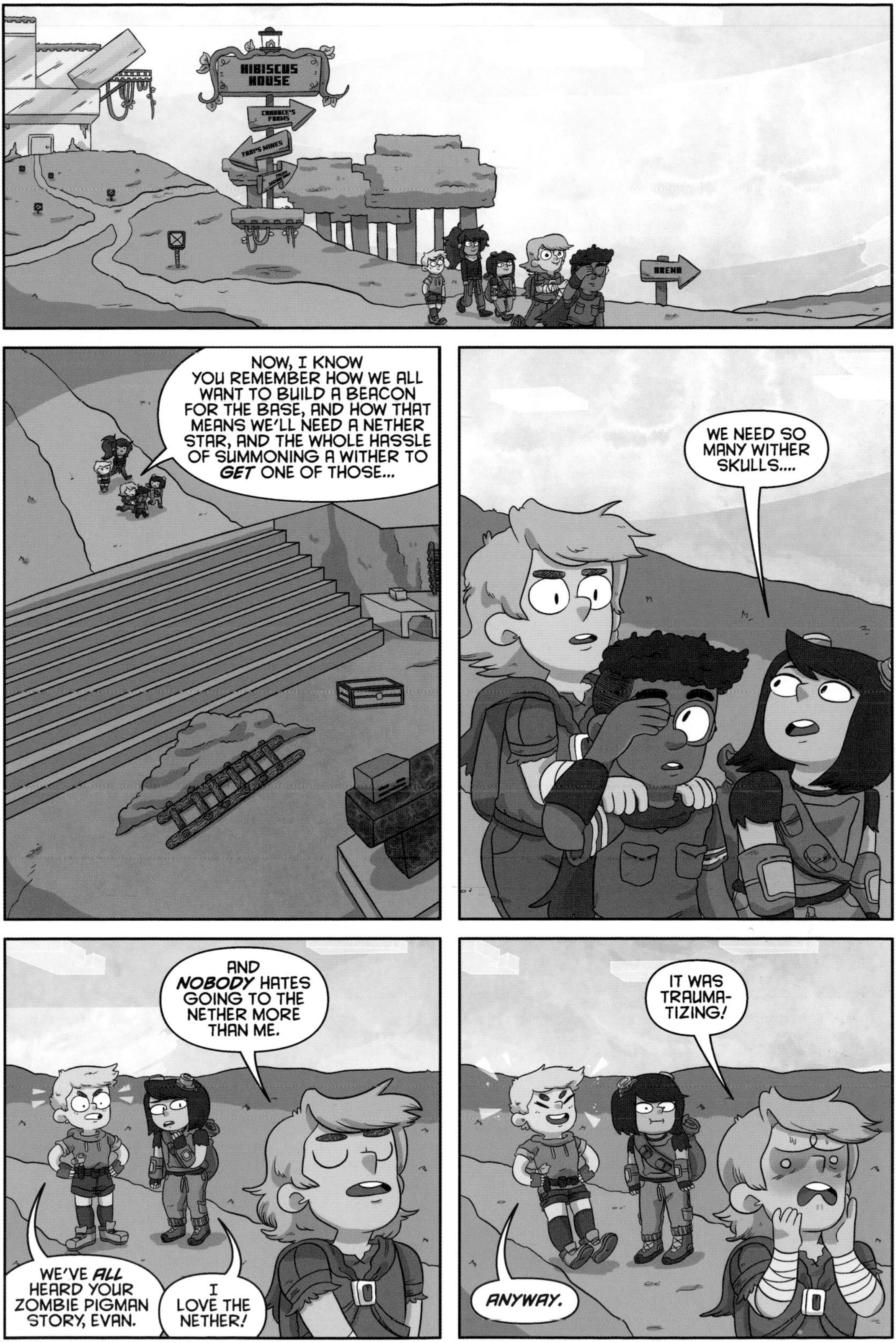
HIBISCUS HOUSE
CANDACE'S FARMS
TOBI'S MINES
ARENA
NOW, I KNOW YOU REMEMBER HOW WE ALL WANT TO BUILD A BEACON FOR THE BASE, AND HOW THAT MEANS WE'LL NEED A NETHER STAR, AND THE WHOLE HASSLE OF SUMMONING A WITHER TO *GET* ONE OF THOSE...
WE NEED SO MANY WITHER SKULLS....
AND *NOBODY* HATES GOING TO THE NETHER MORE THAN ME.
WE'VE *ALL* HEARD YOUR ZOMBIE PIGMAN STORY, EVAN.
I LOVE THE NETHER!
IT WAS TRAUMA-TIZING!
ANYWAY.

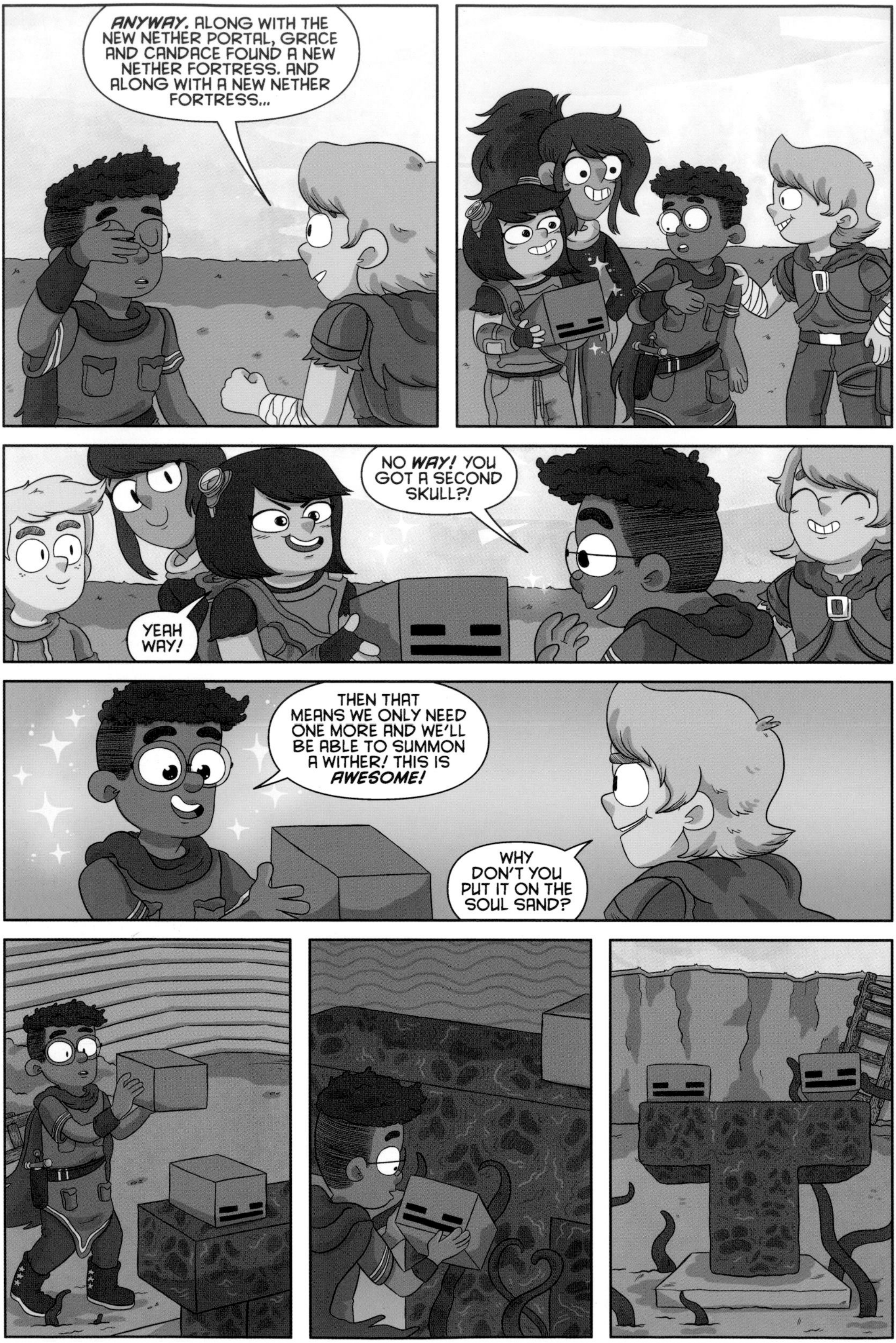
ANYWAY. ALONG WITH THE NEW NETHER PORTAL, GRACE AND CANDACE FOUND A NEW NETHER FORTRESS. AND ALONG WITH A NEW NETHER FORTRESS...
NO WAY! YOU GOT A SECOND SKULL?!
YEAH WAY!
THEN THAT MEANS WE ONLY NEED ONE MORE AND WE'LL BE ABLE TO SUMMON A WITHER! THIS IS AWESOME!
WHY DON'T YOU PUT IT ON THE SOUL SAND?

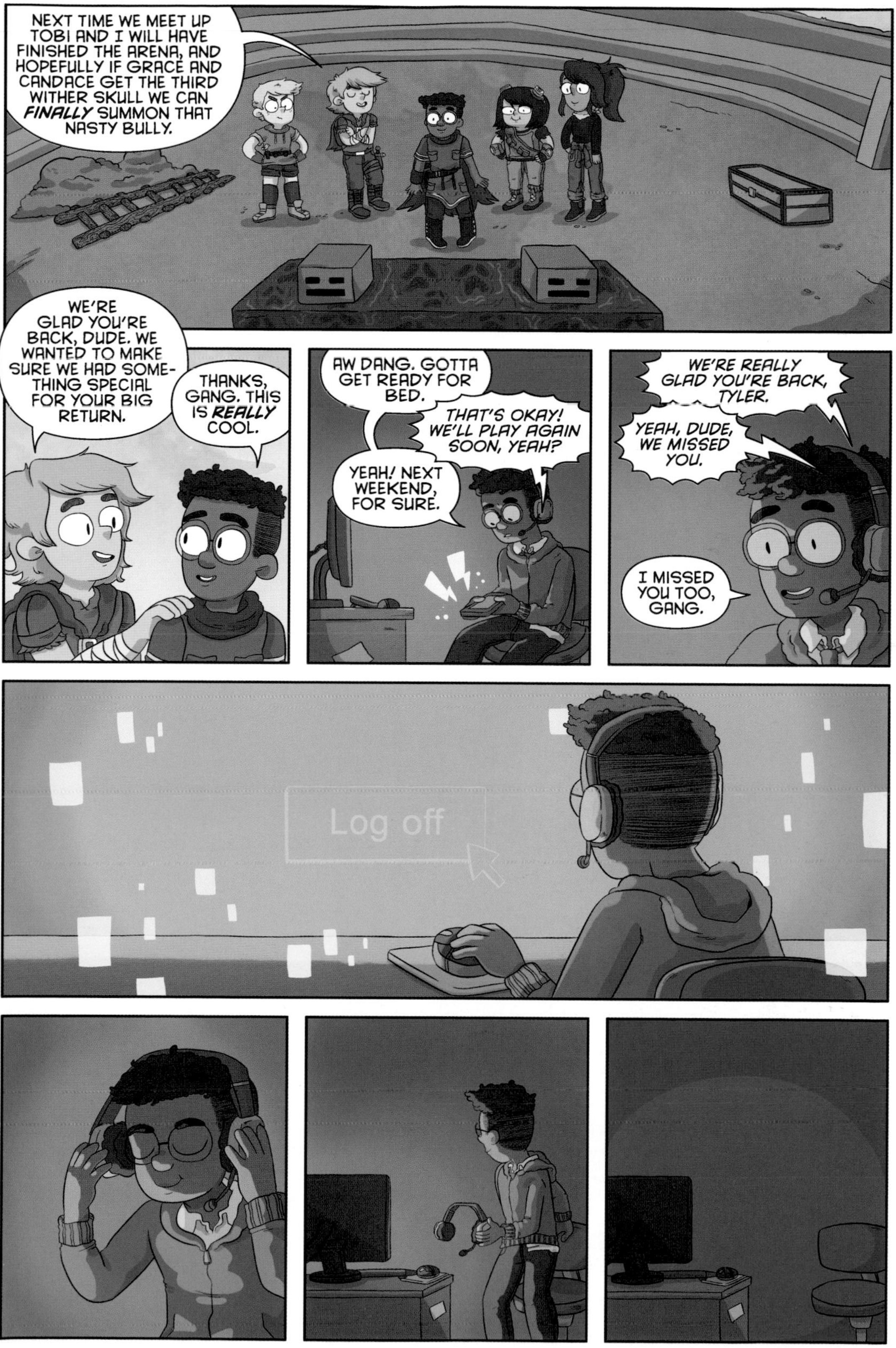

NEXT TIME WE MEET UP TOBI AND I WILL HAVE FINISHED THE ARENA, AND HOPEFULLY IF GRACE AND CANDACE GET THE THIRD WITHER SKULL WE CAN *FINALLY* SUMMON THAT NASTY BULLY.
WE'RE GLAD YOU'RE BACK, DUDE. WE WANTED TO MAKE SURE WE HAD SOMETHING SPECIAL FOR YOUR BIG RETURN.
THANKS, GANG. THIS IS *REALLY* COOL.
AW DANG. GOTTA GET READY FOR BED.
THAT'S OKAY! WE'LL PLAY AGAIN SOON, YEAH?
YEAH! NEXT WEEKEND, FOR SURE.
WE'RE REALLY GLAD YOU'RE BACK, TYLER.
YEAH, DUDE, WE MISSED YOU.
I MISSED YOU TOO, GANG.
Log off

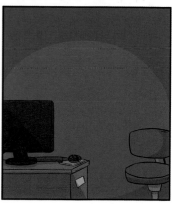

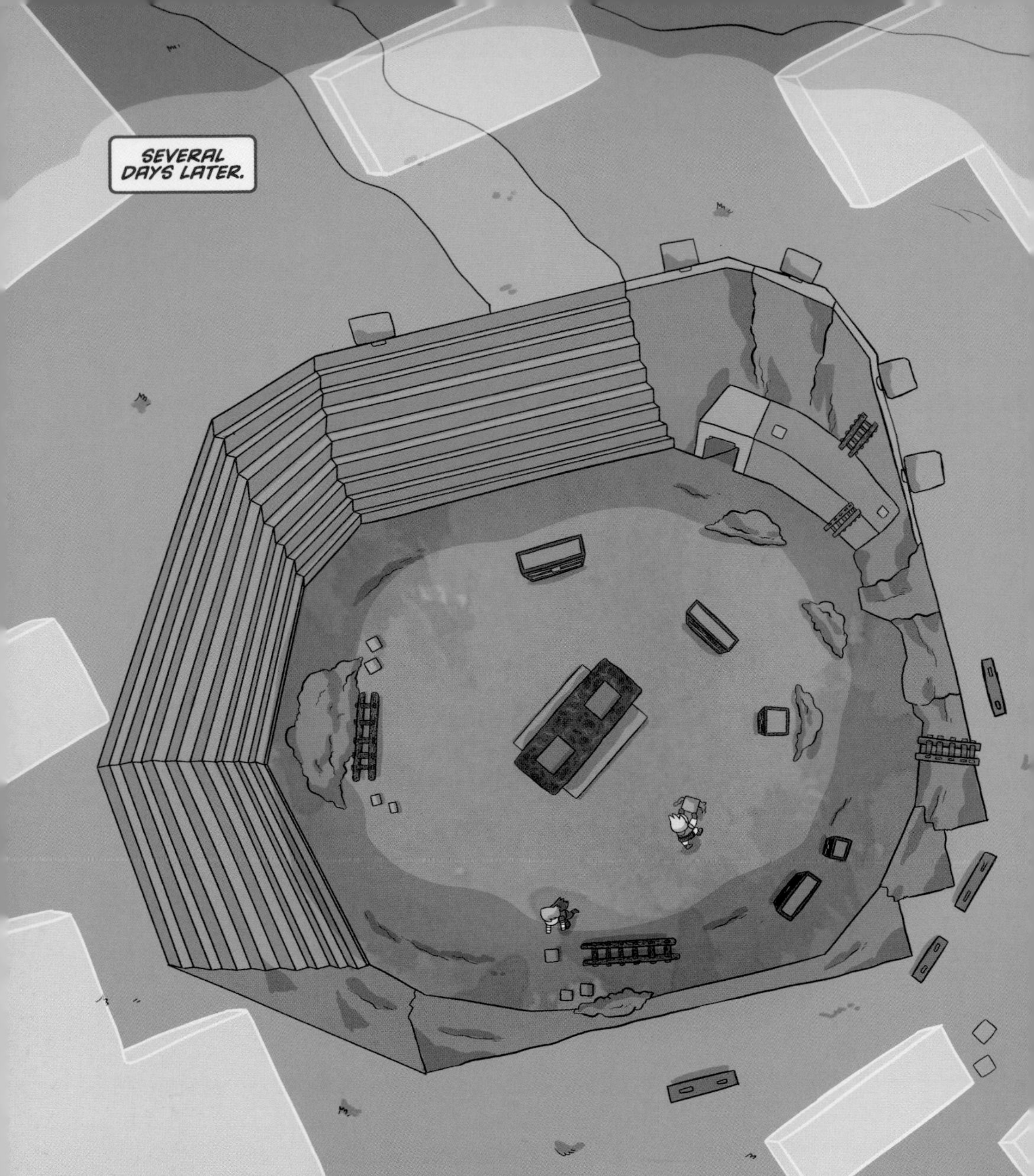
SEVERAL DAYS LATER.

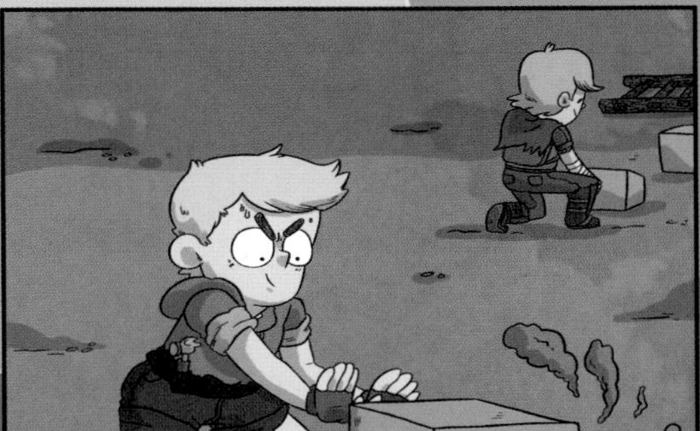

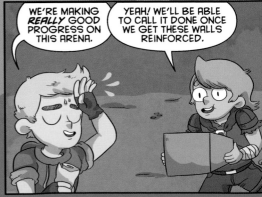

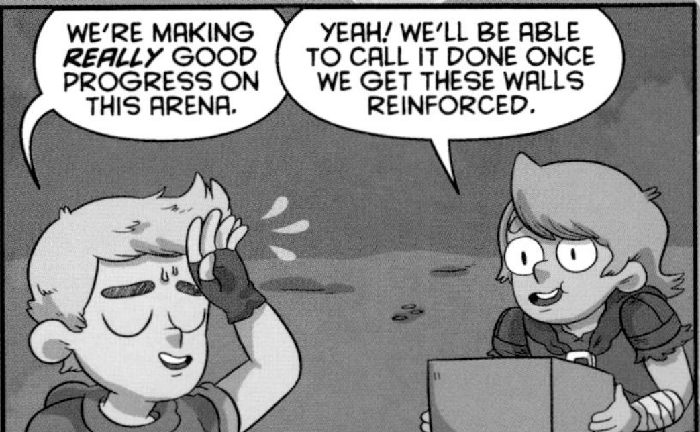
WE'RE MAKING *REALLY* GOOD PROGRESS ON THIS ARENA.
YEAH! WE'LL BE ABLE TO CALL IT DONE ONCE WE GET THESE WALLS REINFORCED.

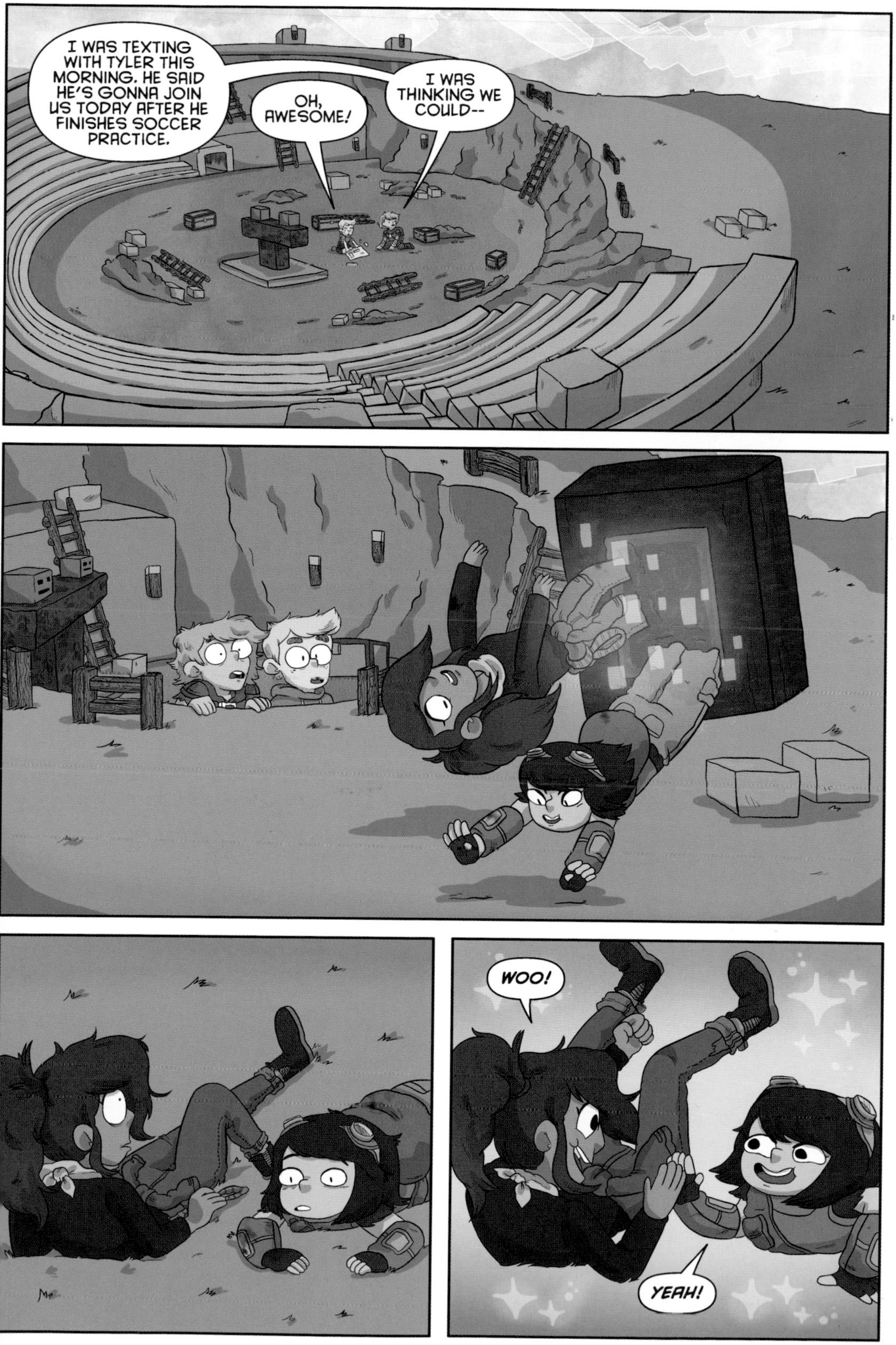
I WAS TEXTING WITH TYLER THIS MORNING. HE SAID HE'S GONNA JOIN US TODAY AFTER HE FINISHES SOCCER PRACTICE.
OH, AWESOME!
I WAS THINKING WE COULD--
WOO!
YEAH!

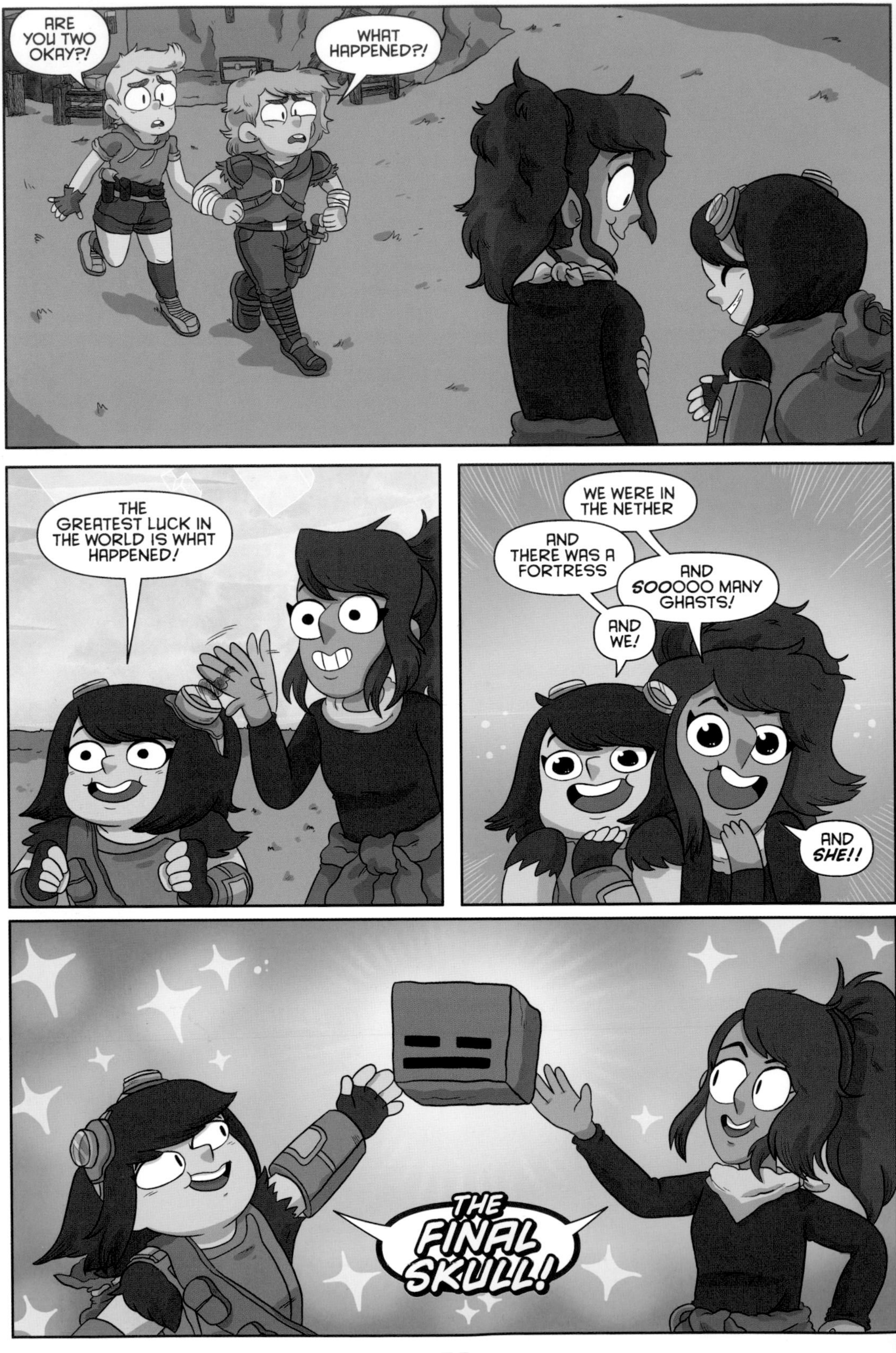
ARE YOU TWO OKAY?!
WHAT HAPPENED?!
THE GREATEST LUCK IN THE WORLD IS WHAT HAPPENED!
WE WERE IN THE NETHER
AND THERE WAS A FORTRESS
AND SOOOOO MANY GHASTS!
AND WE!
AND SHE!!
THE FINAL SKULL!

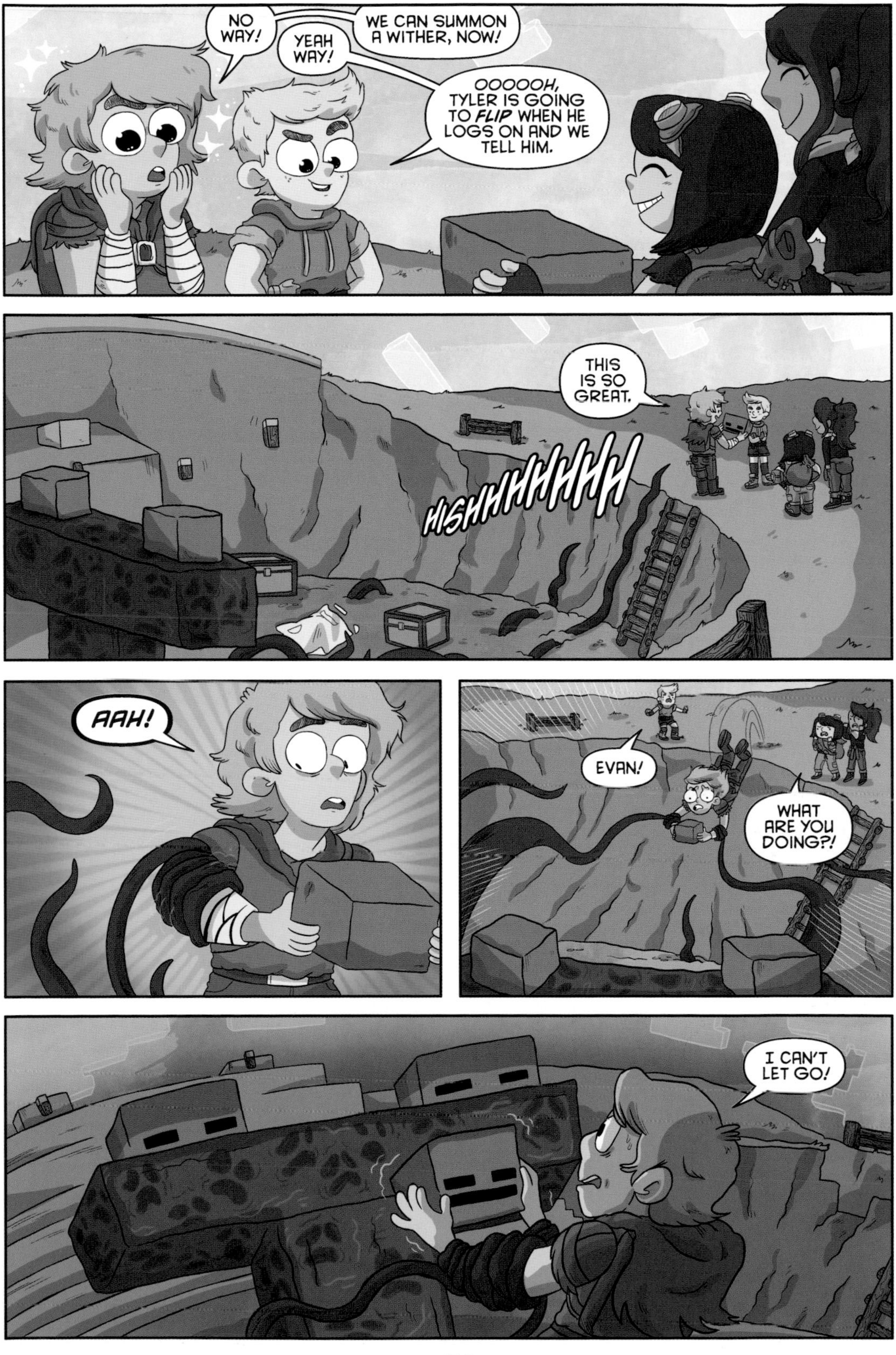
NO WAY!
WE CAN SUMMON A WITHER, NOW!
YEAH WAY!
OOOOOH, TYLER IS GOING TO *FLIP* WHEN HE LOGS ON AND WE TELL HIM.
THIS IS SO GREAT.
HISHHHHHHHHH
AAH!
EVAN!
WHAT ARE YOU DOING?!
I CAN'T LET GO!

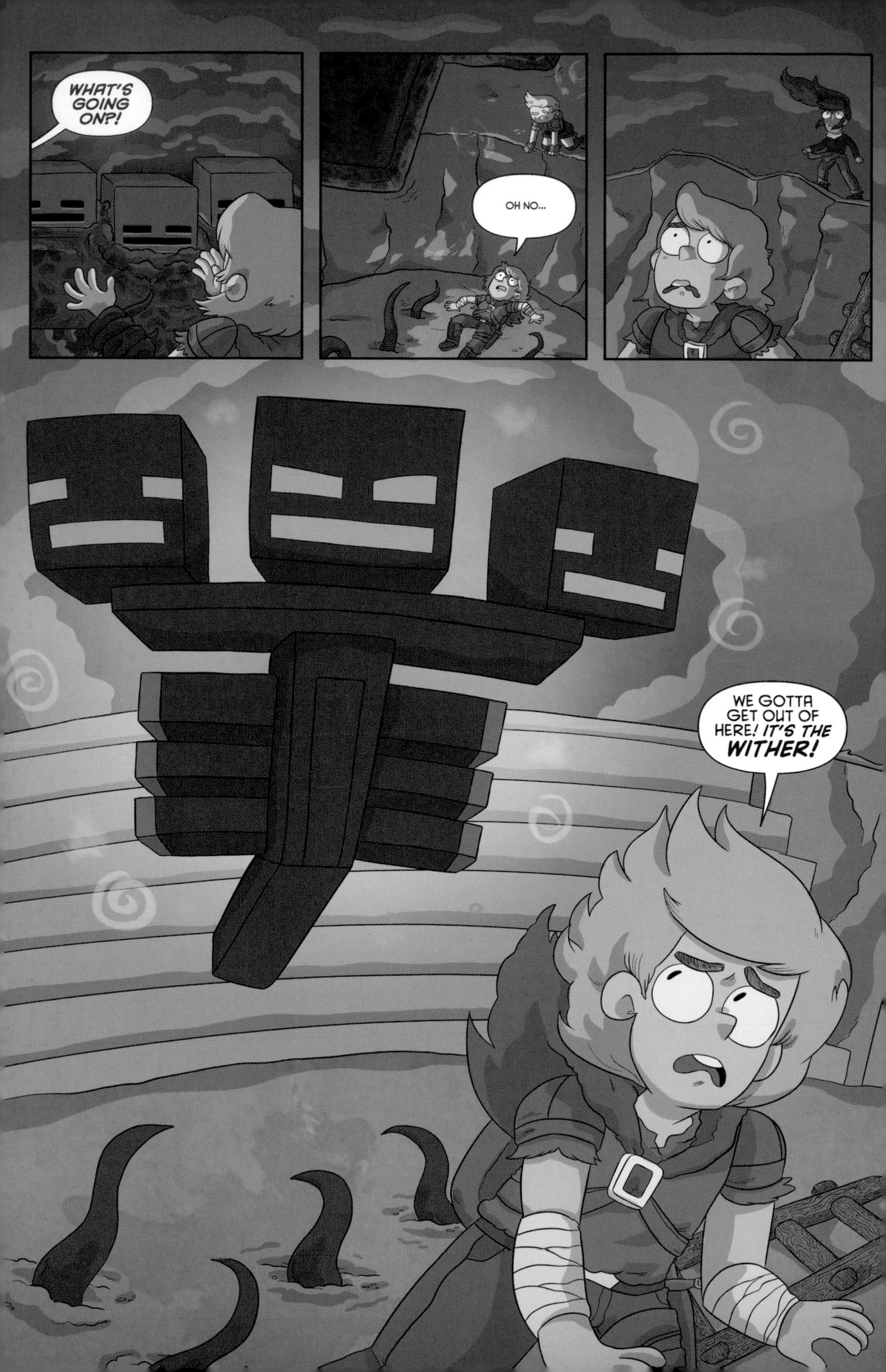
WHAT'S GOING ON?!
OH NO...
WE GOTTA GET OUT OF HERE! IT'S THE WITHER!

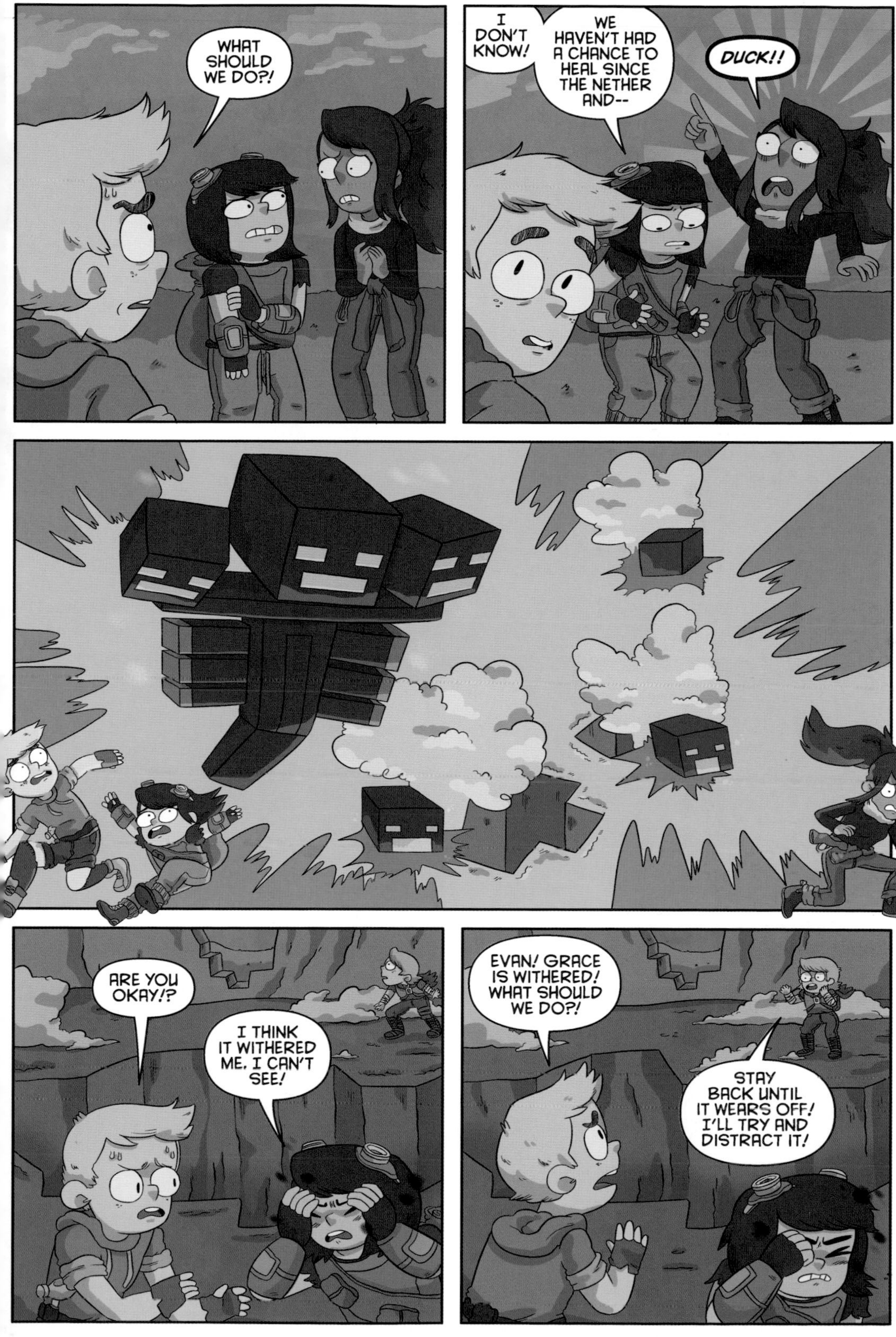
WHAT SHOULD WE DO?!
I DON'T KNOW!
WE HAVEN'T HAD A CHANCE TO HEAL SINCE THE NETHER AND--
DUCK!!
ARE YOU OKAY!?
I THINK IT WITHERED ME. I CAN'T SEE!
EVAN! GRACE IS WITHERED! WHAT SHOULD WE DO?!
STAY BACK UNTIL IT WEARS OFF! I'LL TRY AND DISTRACT IT!

WE CAN'T ATTACK IT IF WE CAN'T GET PAST THOSE EXPLOSIONS!

WE NEED TYLER! *HE'D* KNOW HOW TO--

AAHHH!

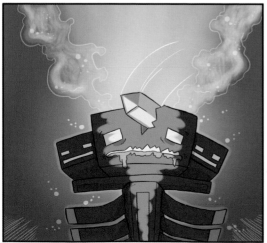

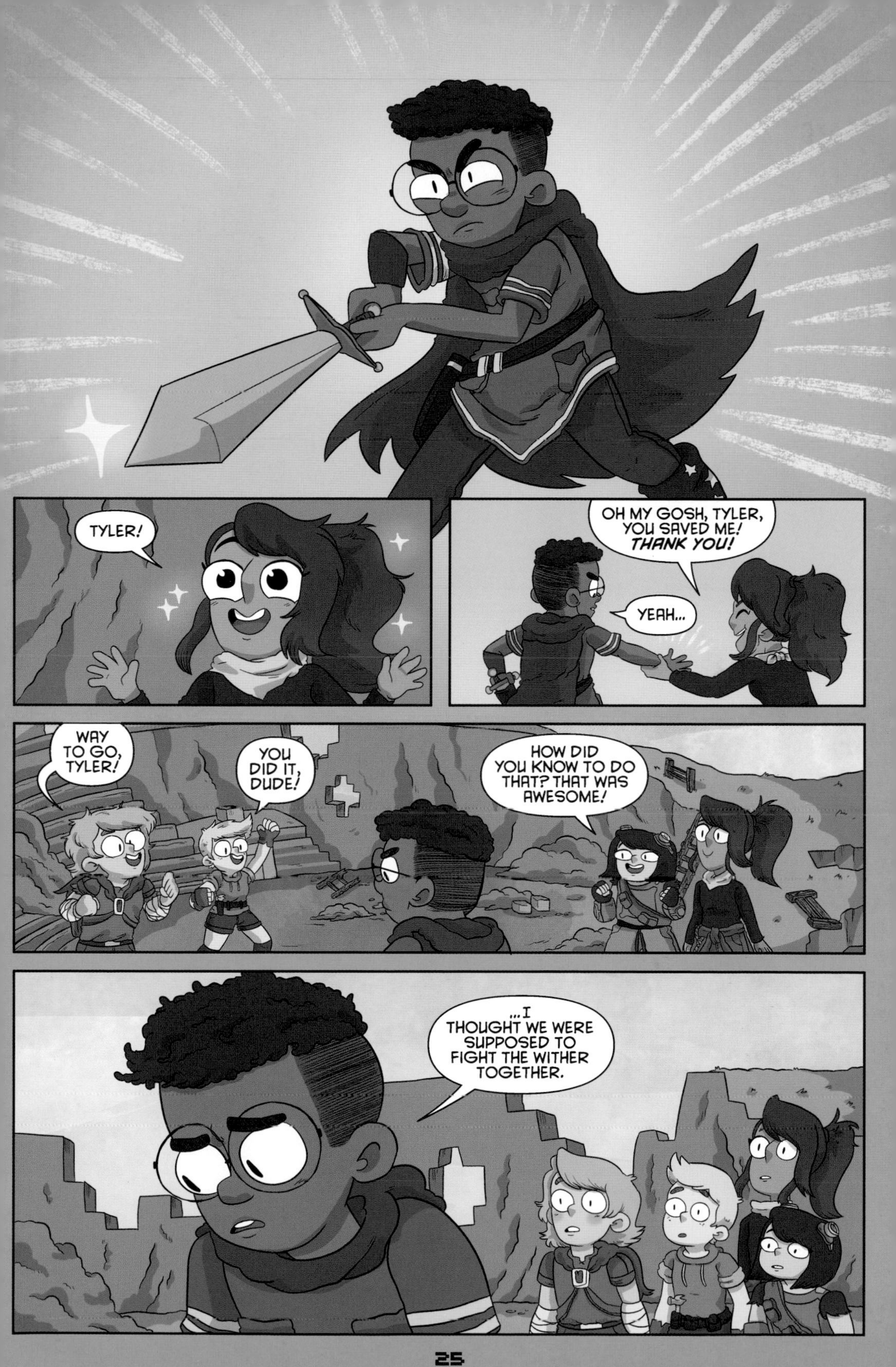
TYLER!
OH MY GOSH, TYLER, YOU SAVED ME! ***THANK YOU!***
YEAH...
WAY TO GO, TYLER!
YOU DID IT, DUDE!
HOW DID YOU KNOW TO DO THAT? THAT WAS AWESOME!
...I THOUGHT WE WERE SUPPOSED TO FIGHT THE WITHER TOGETHER.

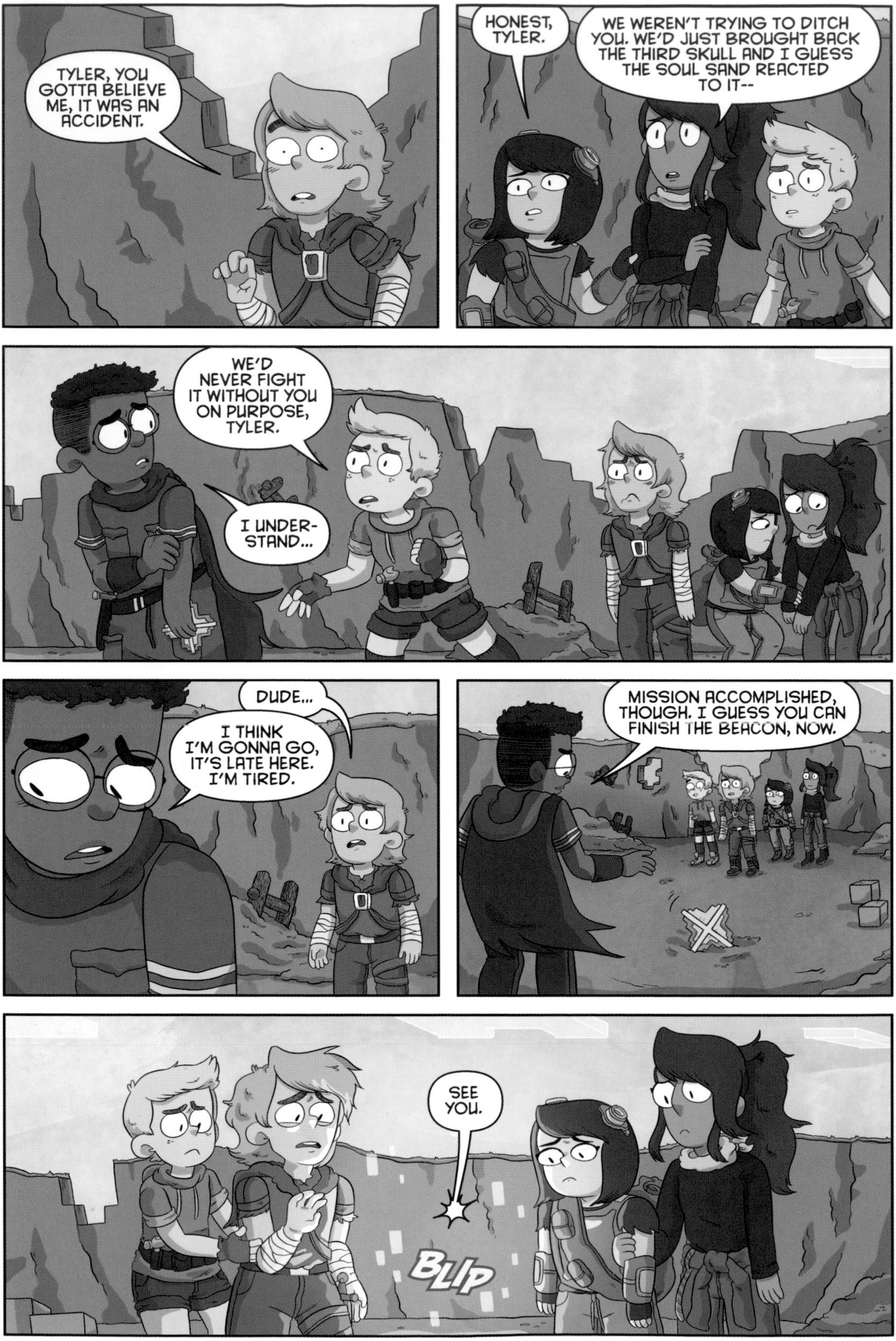
TYLER, YOU GOTTA BELIEVE ME, IT WAS AN ACCIDENT.
HONEST, TYLER.
WE WEREN'T TRYING TO DITCH YOU. WE'D JUST BROUGHT BACK THE THIRD SKULL AND I GUESS THE SOUL SAND REACTED TO IT--
WE'D NEVER FIGHT IT WITHOUT YOU ON PURPOSE, TYLER.
I UNDER-STAND...
DUDE...
I THINK I'M GONNA GO, IT'S LATE HERE. I'M TIRED.
MISSION ACCOMPLISHED, THOUGH. I GUESS YOU CAN FINISH THE BEACON, NOW.
SEE YOU.
BLIP

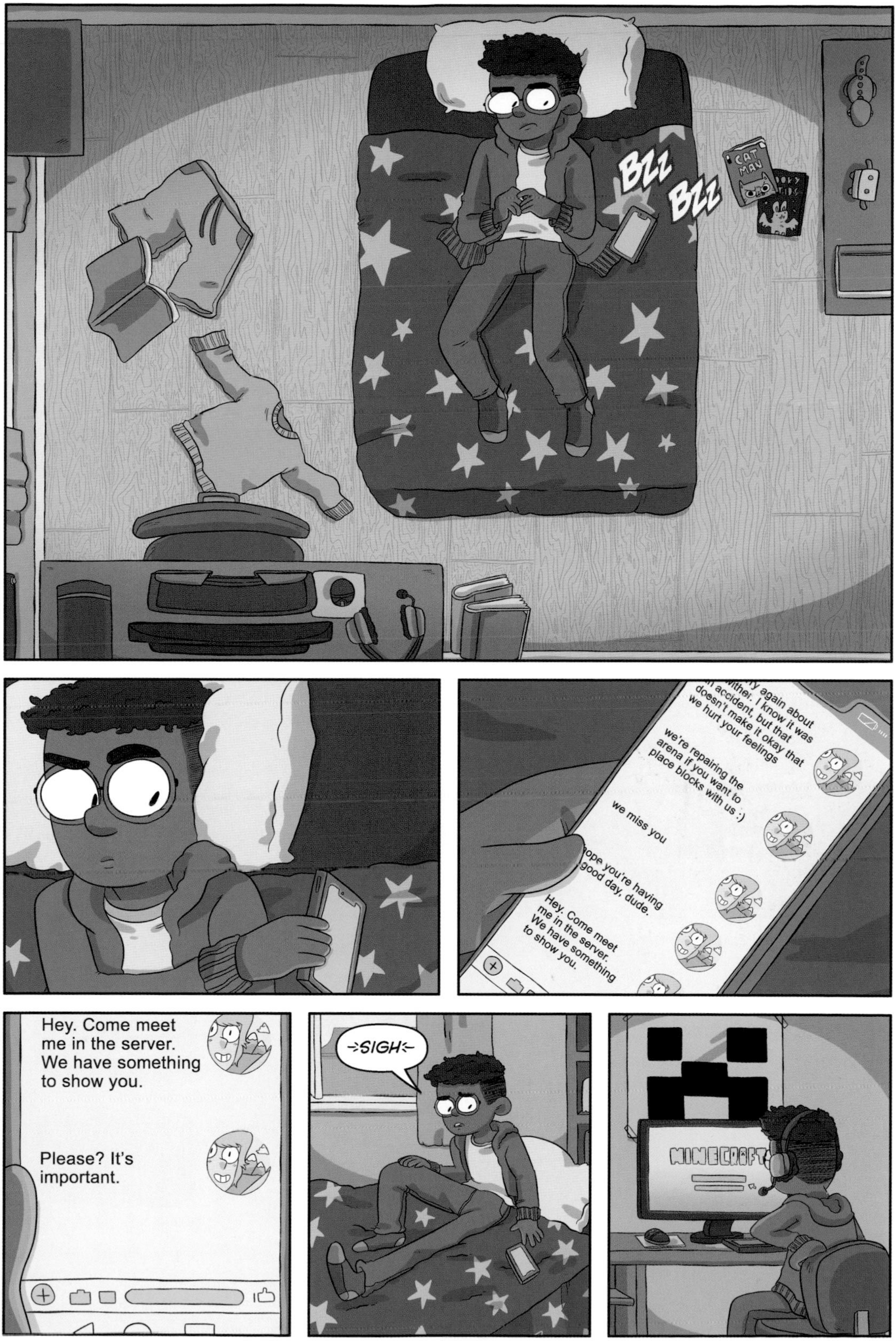
BZZ BZZ
CAT MAN
again about
I know it was
accident, but that
doesn't make it okay that
we hurt your feelings
we're repairing the
arena if you want to
place blocks with us :)
we miss you
good day, dude.
Hey. Come meet
me in the server.
We have something
to show you.
Hey. Come meet
me in the server.
We have something
to show you.
Please? It's
important.
SIGH
MINECRAFT

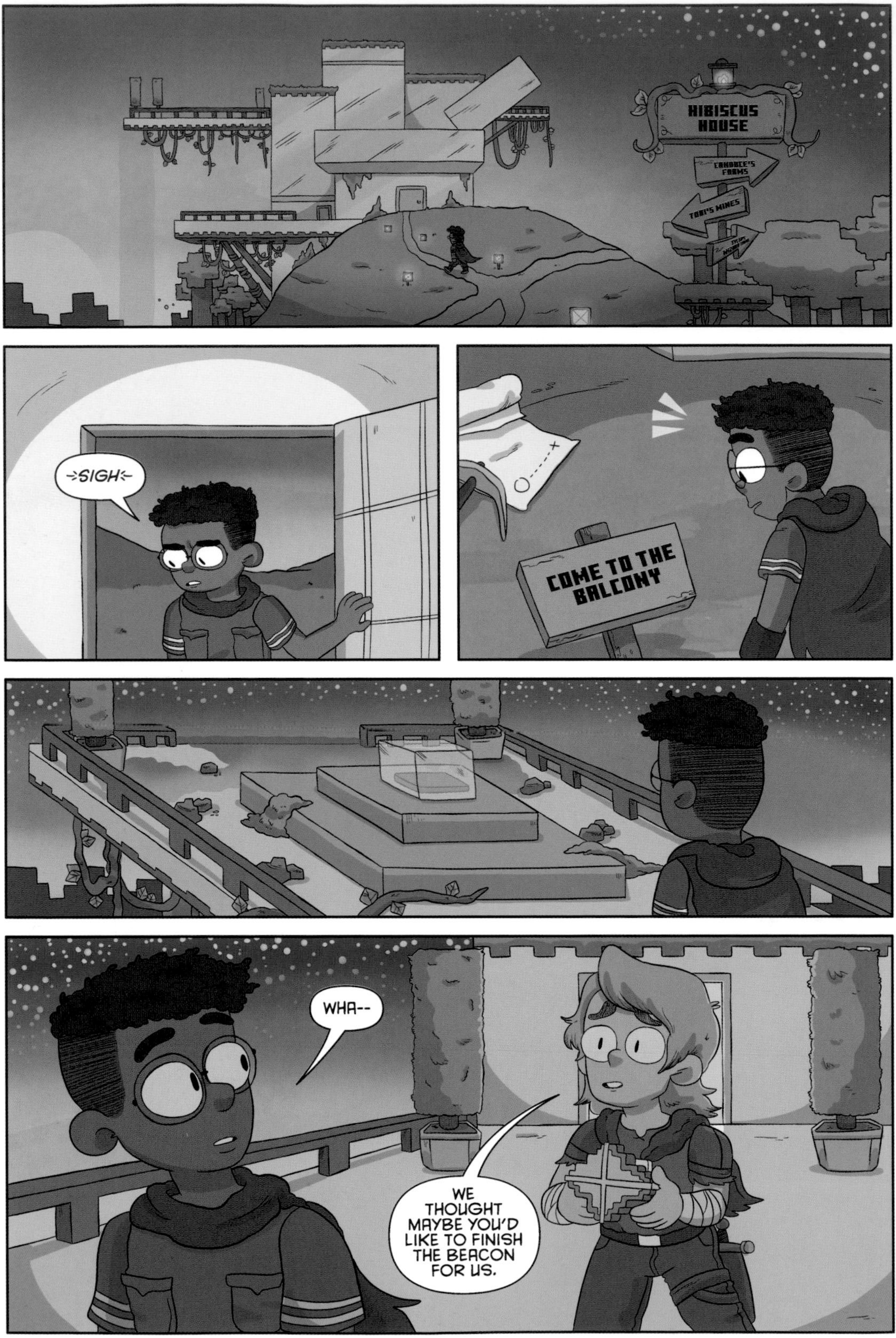
HIBISCUS HOUSE
CANDACE'S FARMS
TOBI'S MINES
SIGH
COME TO THE BALCONY
WHA--
WE THOUGHT MAYBE YOU'D LIKE TO FINISH THE BEACON FOR US.

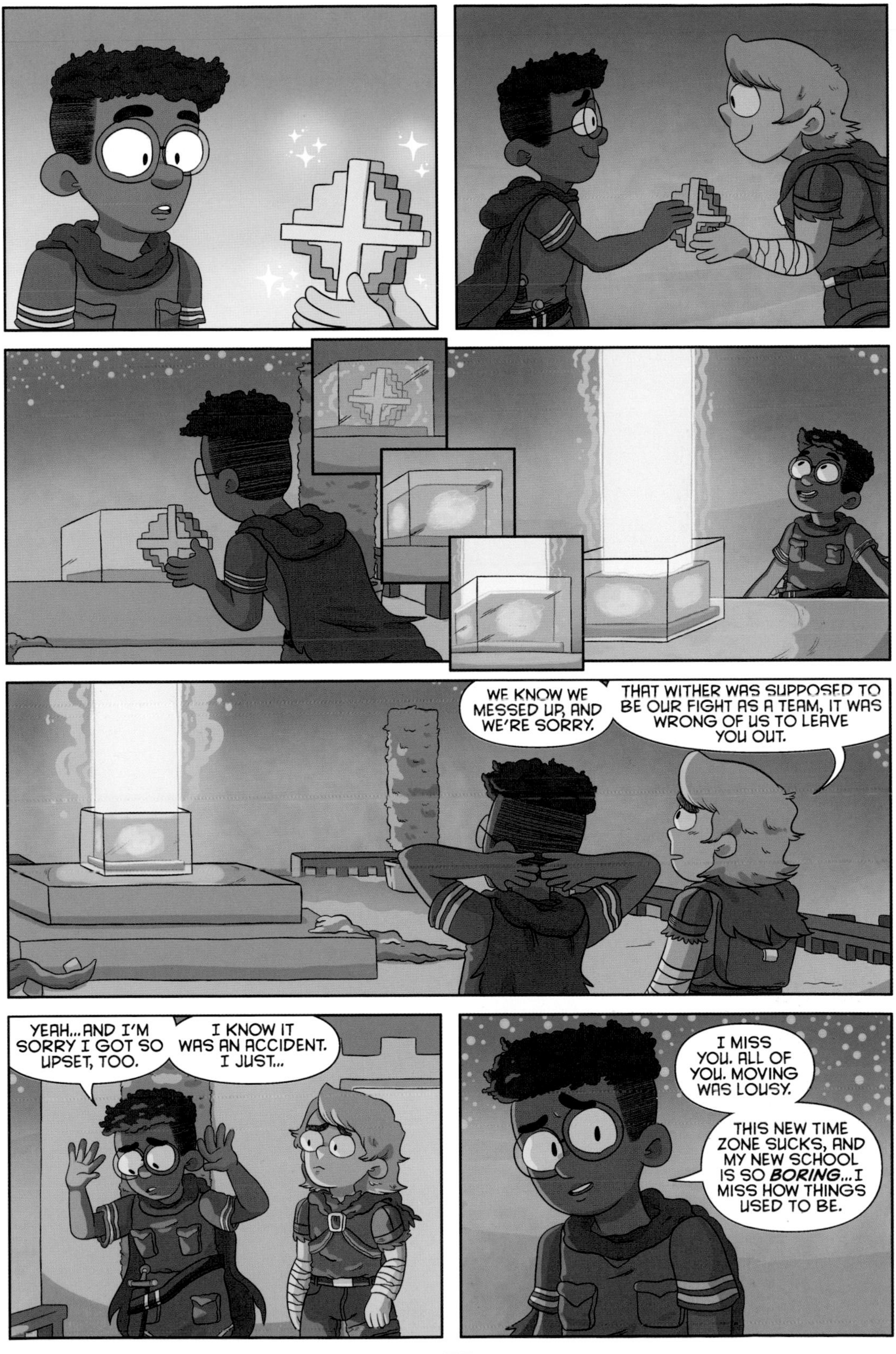
WE KNOW WE MESSED UP, AND WE'RE SORRY.
THAT WITHER WAS SUPPOSED TO BE OUR FIGHT AS A TEAM, IT WAS WRONG OF US TO LEAVE YOU OUT.
YEAH... AND I'M SORRY I GOT SO UPSET, TOO.
I KNOW IT WAS AN ACCIDENT. I JUST...
I MISS YOU. ALL OF YOU. MOVING WAS LOUSY.
THIS NEW TIME ZONE SUCKS, AND MY NEW SCHOOL IS SO ***BORING***... I MISS HOW THINGS USED TO BE.

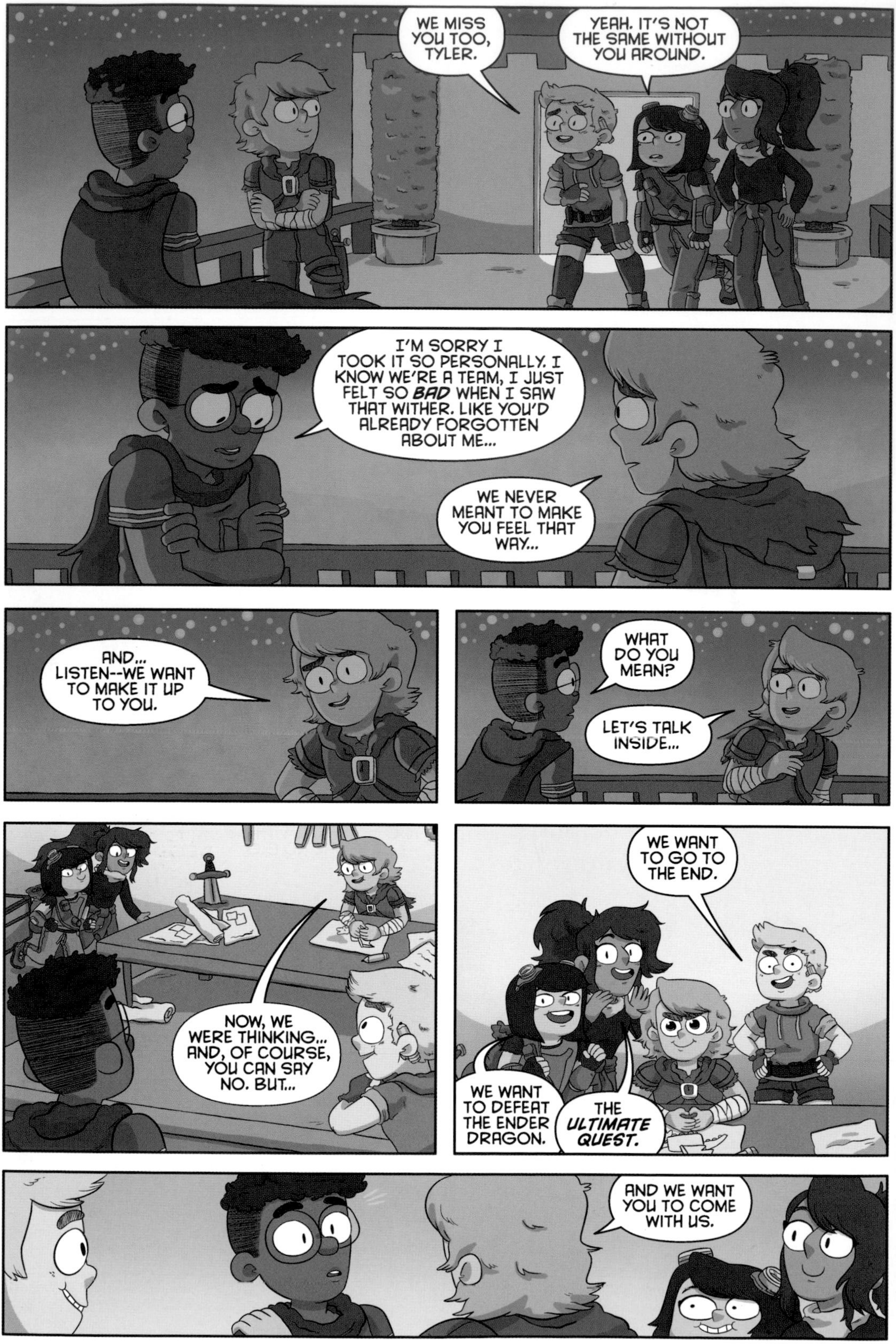
WE MISS YOU TOO, TYLER.
YEAH. IT'S NOT THE SAME WITHOUT YOU AROUND.
I'M SORRY I TOOK IT SO PERSONALLY. I KNOW WE'RE A TEAM, I JUST FELT SO *BAD* WHEN I SAW THAT WITHER. LIKE YOU'D ALREADY FORGOTTEN ABOUT ME...
WE NEVER MEANT TO MAKE YOU FEEL THAT WAY...
AND... LISTEN--WE WANT TO MAKE IT UP TO YOU.
WHAT DO YOU MEAN?
LET'S TALK INSIDE...
NOW, WE WERE THINKING... AND, OF COURSE, YOU CAN SAY NO. BUT...
WE WANT TO GO TO THE END.
WE WANT TO DEFEAT THE ENDER DRAGON.
THE *ULTIMATE QUEST.*
AND WE WANT YOU TO COME WITH US.

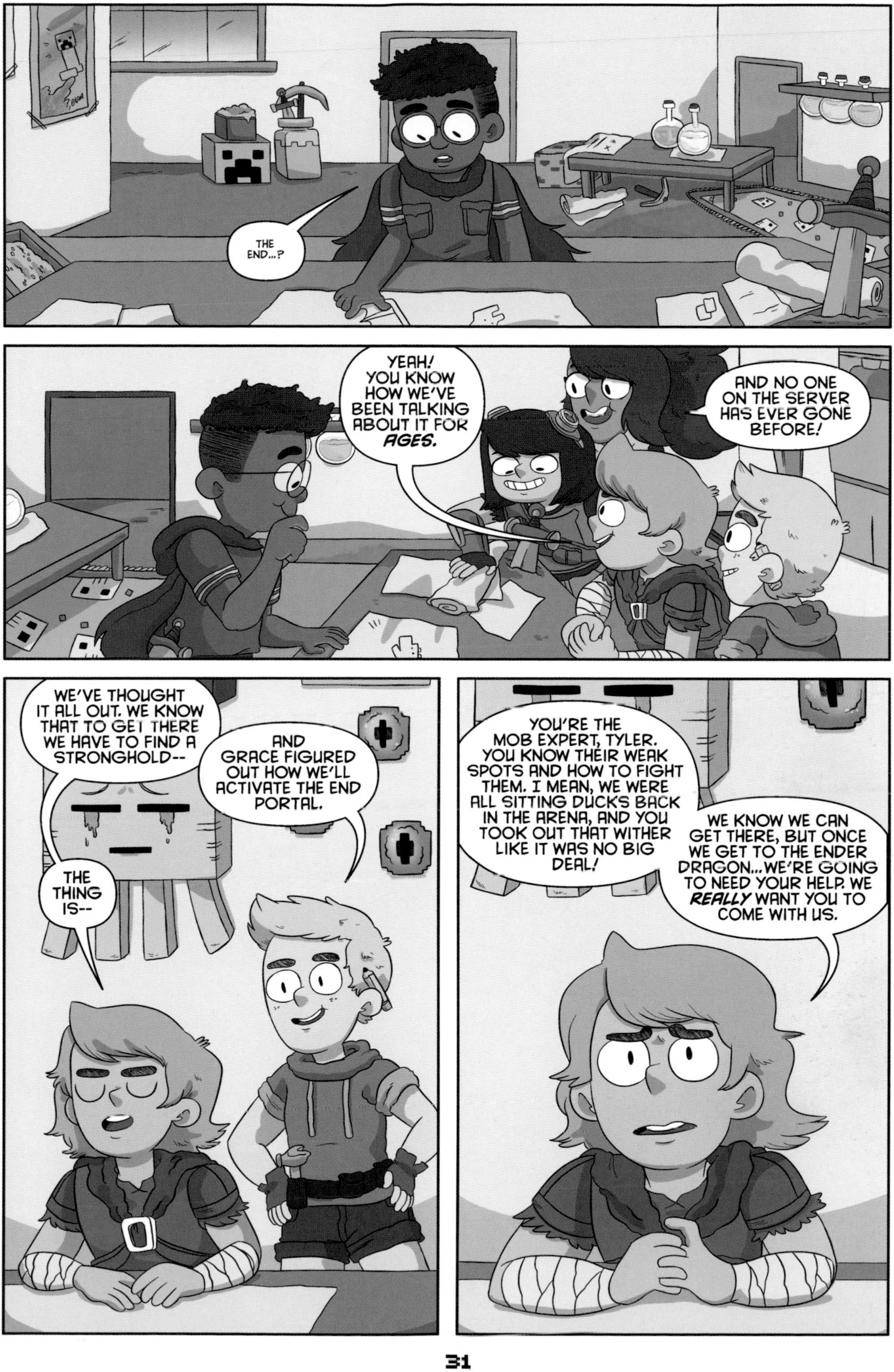
THE END...?
YEAH! YOU KNOW HOW WE'VE BEEN TALKING ABOUT IT FOR AGES.
AND NO ONE ON THE SERVER HAS EVER GONE BEFORE!
WE'VE THOUGHT IT ALL OUT. WE KNOW THAT TO GET THERE WE HAVE TO FIND A STRONGHOLD--
AND GRACE FIGURED OUT HOW WE'LL ACTIVATE THE END PORTAL.
THE THING IS--
YOU'RE THE MOB EXPERT, TYLER. YOU KNOW THEIR WEAK SPOTS AND HOW TO FIGHT THEM. I MEAN, WE WERE ALL SITTING DUCKS BACK IN THE ARENA, AND YOU TOOK OUT THAT WITHER LIKE IT WAS NO BIG DEAL!
WE KNOW WE CAN GET THERE, BUT ONCE WE GET TO THE ENDER DRAGON...WE'RE GOING TO NEED YOUR HELP. WE REALLY WANT YOU TO COME WITH US.

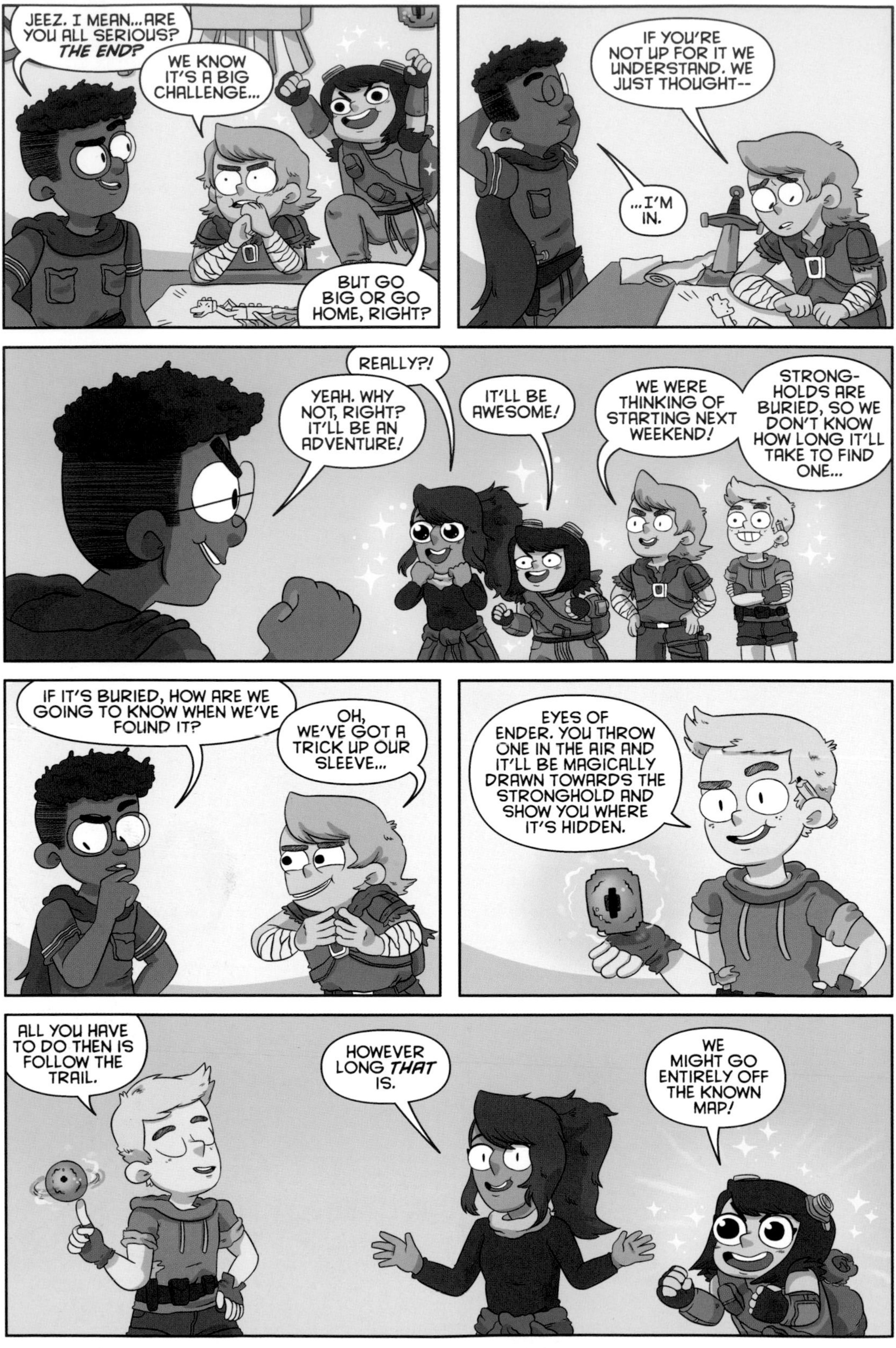
JEEZ. I MEAN...ARE YOU ALL SERIOUS? THE END?
WE KNOW IT'S A BIG CHALLENGE...
BUT GO BIG OR GO HOME, RIGHT?
IF YOU'RE NOT UP FOR IT WE UNDERSTAND. WE JUST THOUGHT--
...I'M IN.
REALLY?!
YEAH. WHY NOT, RIGHT? IT'LL BE AN ADVENTURE!
IT'LL BE AWESOME!
WE WERE THINKING OF STARTING NEXT WEEKEND!
STRONGHOLDS ARE BURIED, SO WE DON'T KNOW HOW LONG IT'LL TAKE TO FIND ONE...
IF IT'S BURIED, HOW ARE WE GOING TO KNOW WHEN WE'VE FOUND IT?
OH, WE'VE GOT A TRICK UP OUR SLEEVE...
EYES OF ENDER. YOU THROW ONE IN THE AIR AND IT'LL BE MAGICALLY DRAWN TOWARDS THE STRONGHOLD AND SHOW YOU WHERE IT'S HIDDEN.
ALL YOU HAVE TO DO THEN IS FOLLOW THE TRAIL.
HOWEVER LONG THAT IS.
WE MIGHT GO ENTIRELY OFF THE KNOWN MAP!

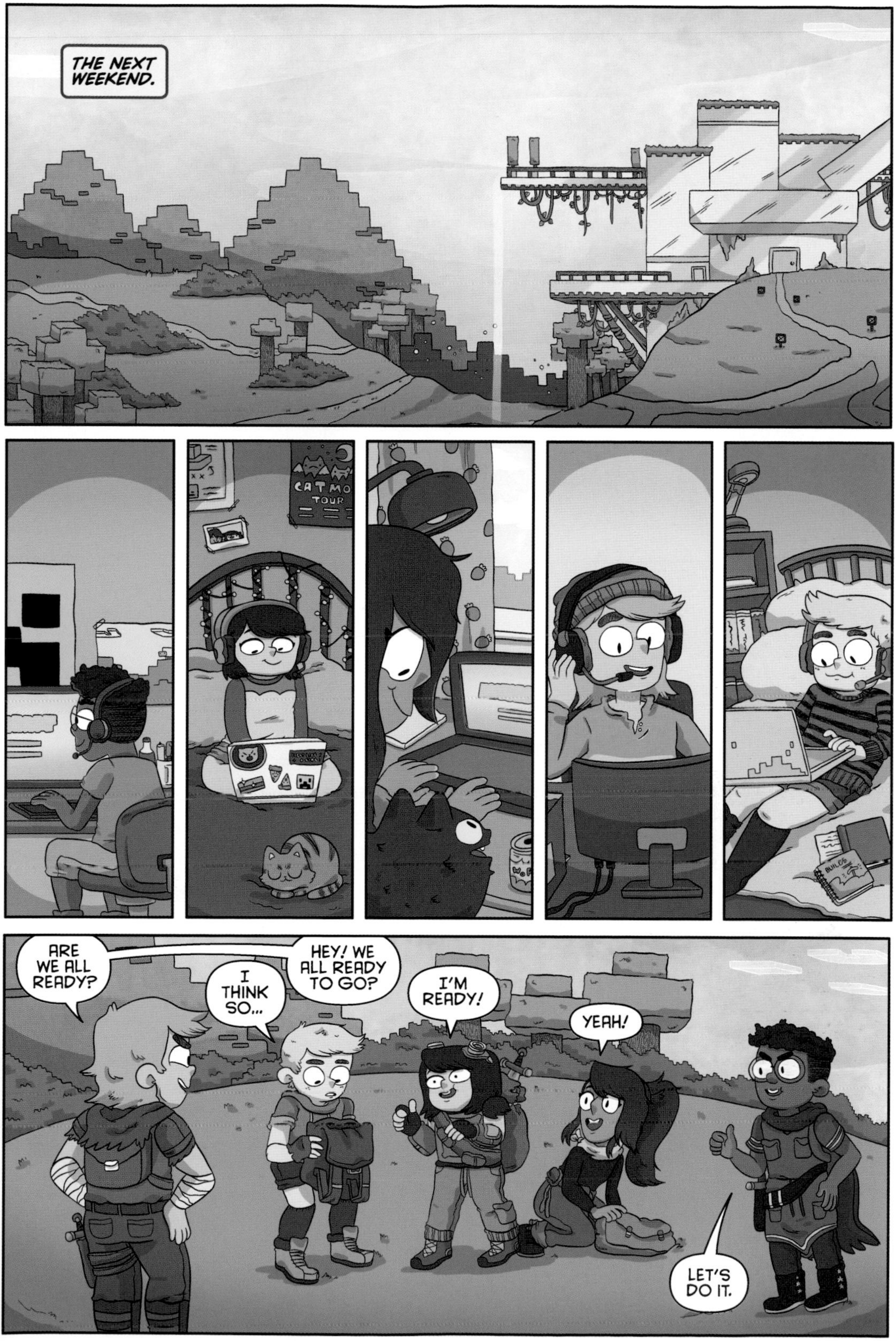
THE NEXT WEEKEND.
CATMO
TOUR
ARE WE ALL READY?
I THINK SO...
HEY! WE ALL READY TO GO?
I'M READY!
YEAH!
LET'S DO IT.

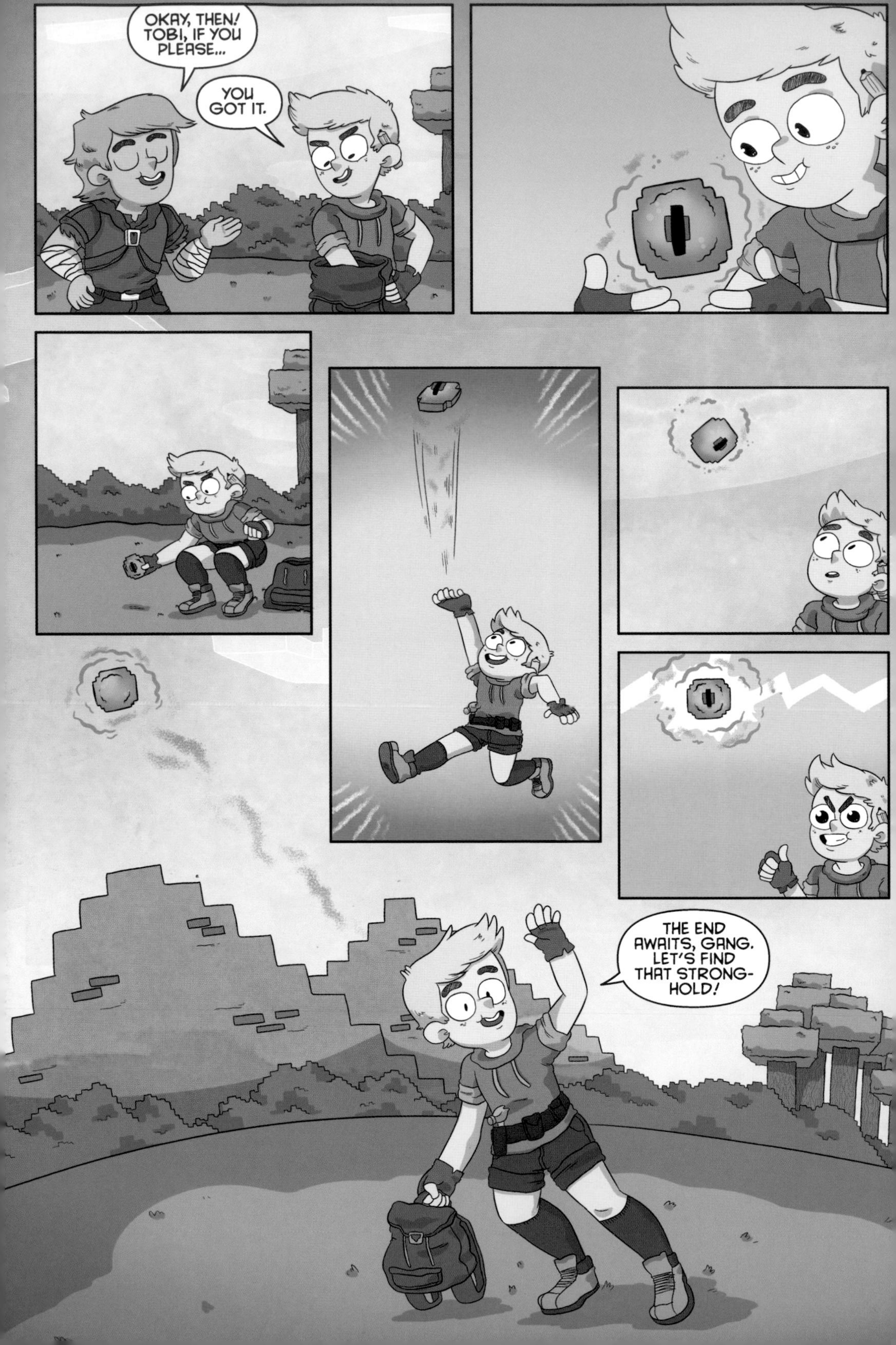
OKAY, THEN! TOBI, IF YOU PLEASE...
YOU GOT IT.
THE END AWAITS, GANG. LET'S FIND THAT STRONG-HOLD!

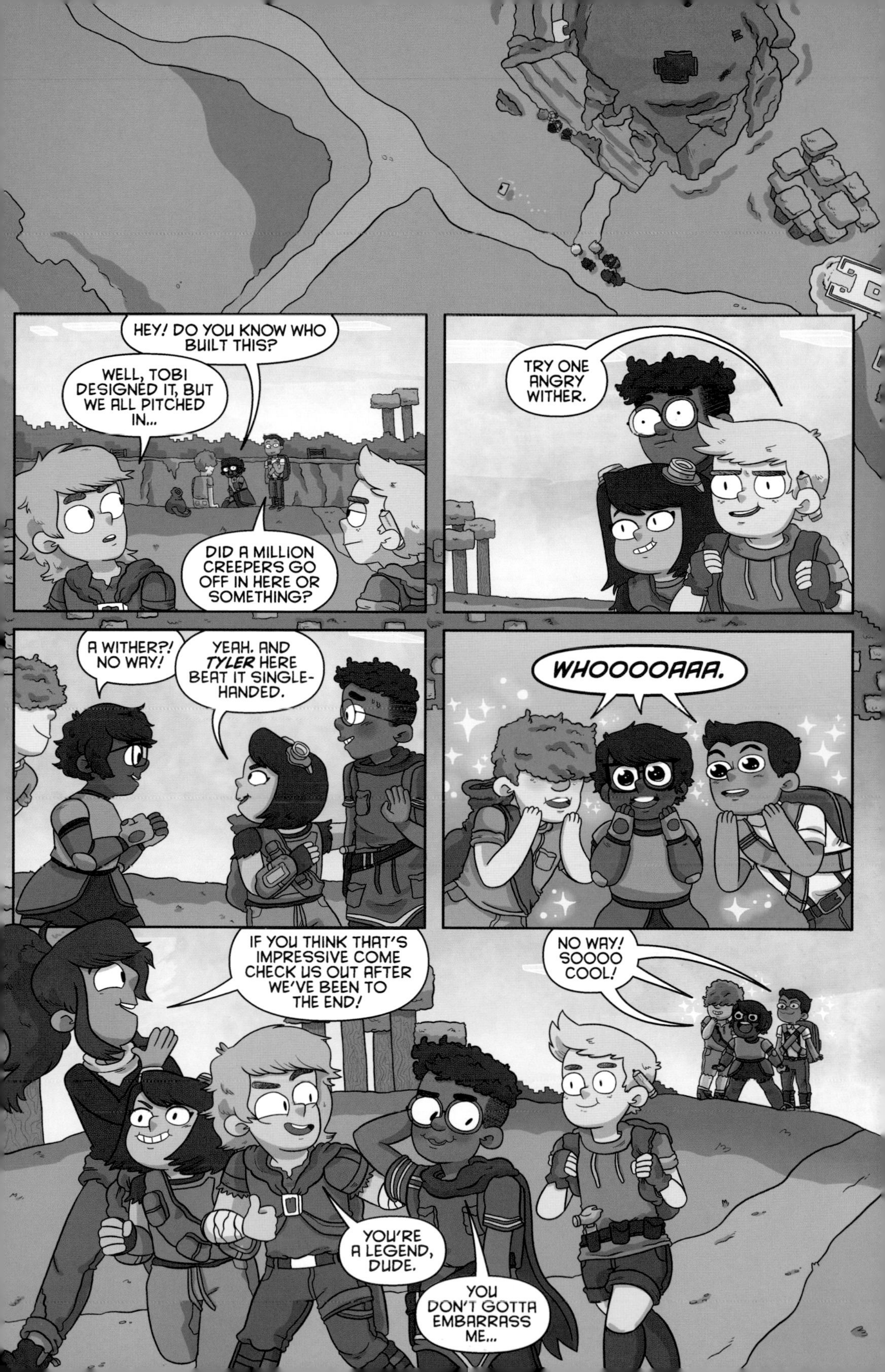

HEY! DO YOU KNOW WHO BUILT THIS?
WELL, TOBI DESIGNED IT, BUT WE ALL PITCHED IN...
DID A MILLION CREEPERS GO OFF IN HERE OR SOMETHING?
TRY ONE ANGRY WITHER.
A WITHER?! NO WAY!
YEAH. AND *TYLER* HERE BEAT IT SINGLE-HANDED.
WHOOOOAAA.
IF YOU THINK THAT'S IMPRESSIVE COME CHECK US OUT AFTER WE'VE BEEN TO THE END!
NO WAY! SOOOO COOL!
YOU'RE A LEGEND, DUDE.
YOU DON'T GOTTA EMBARRASS ME...

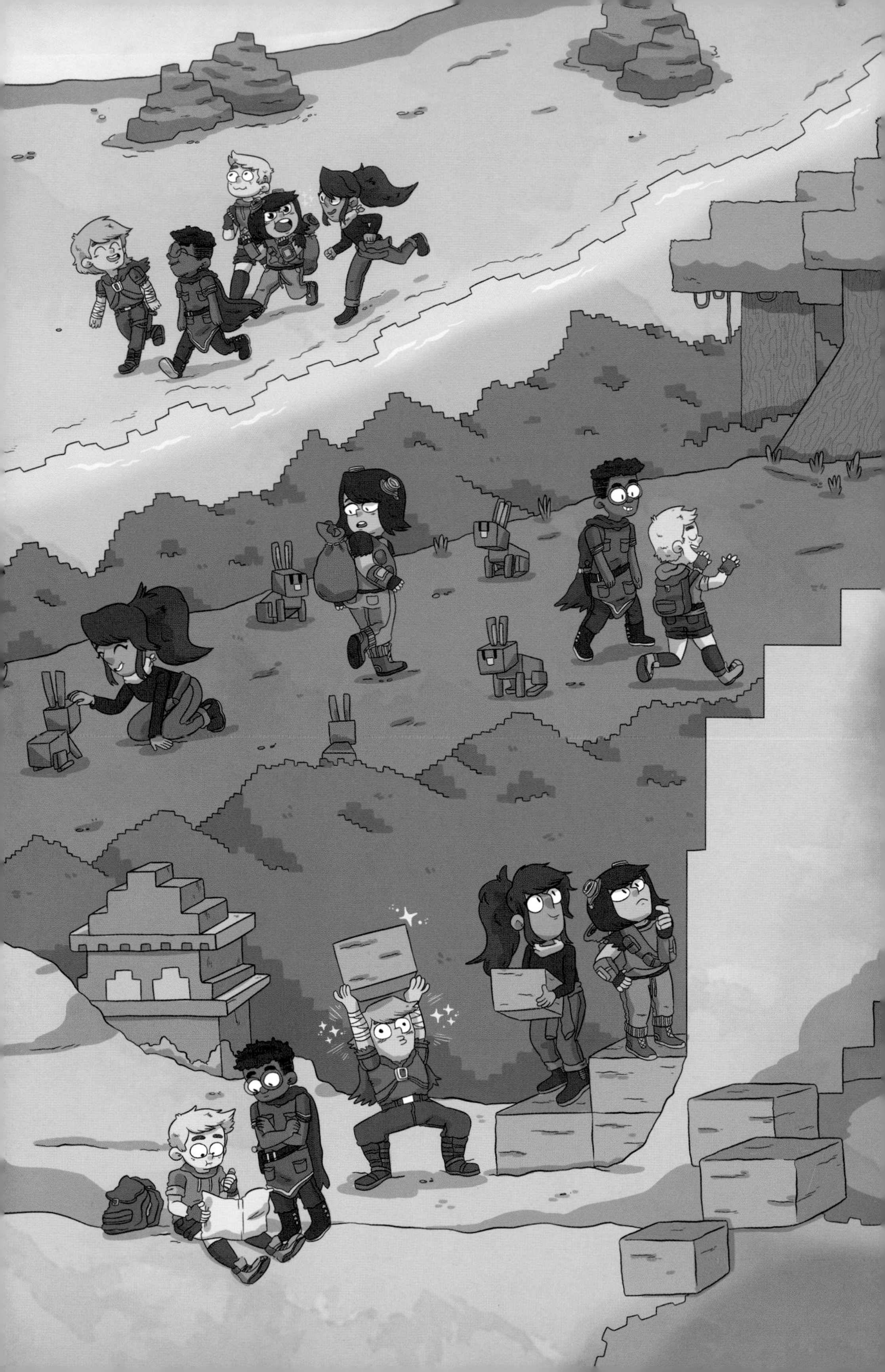

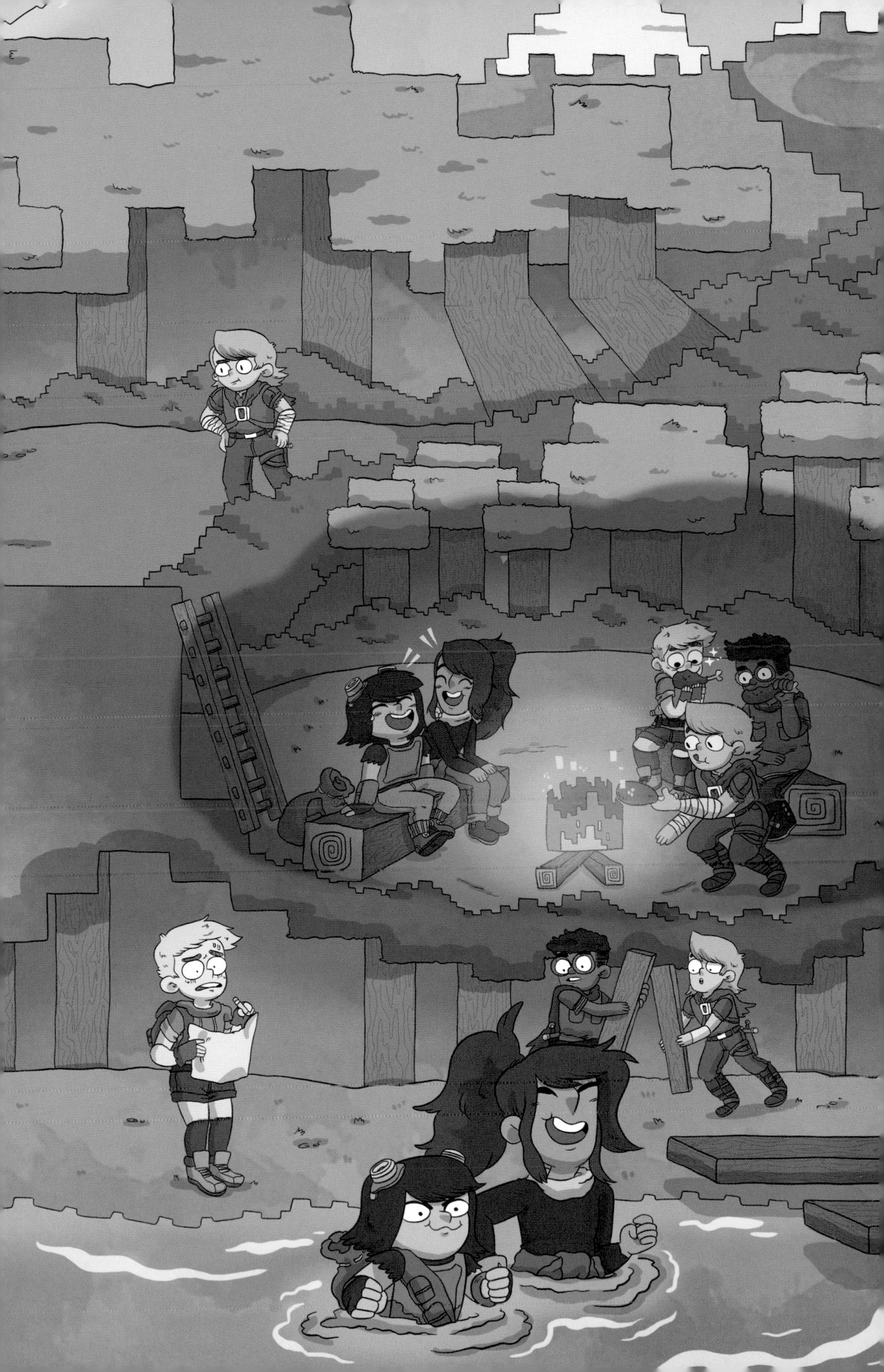

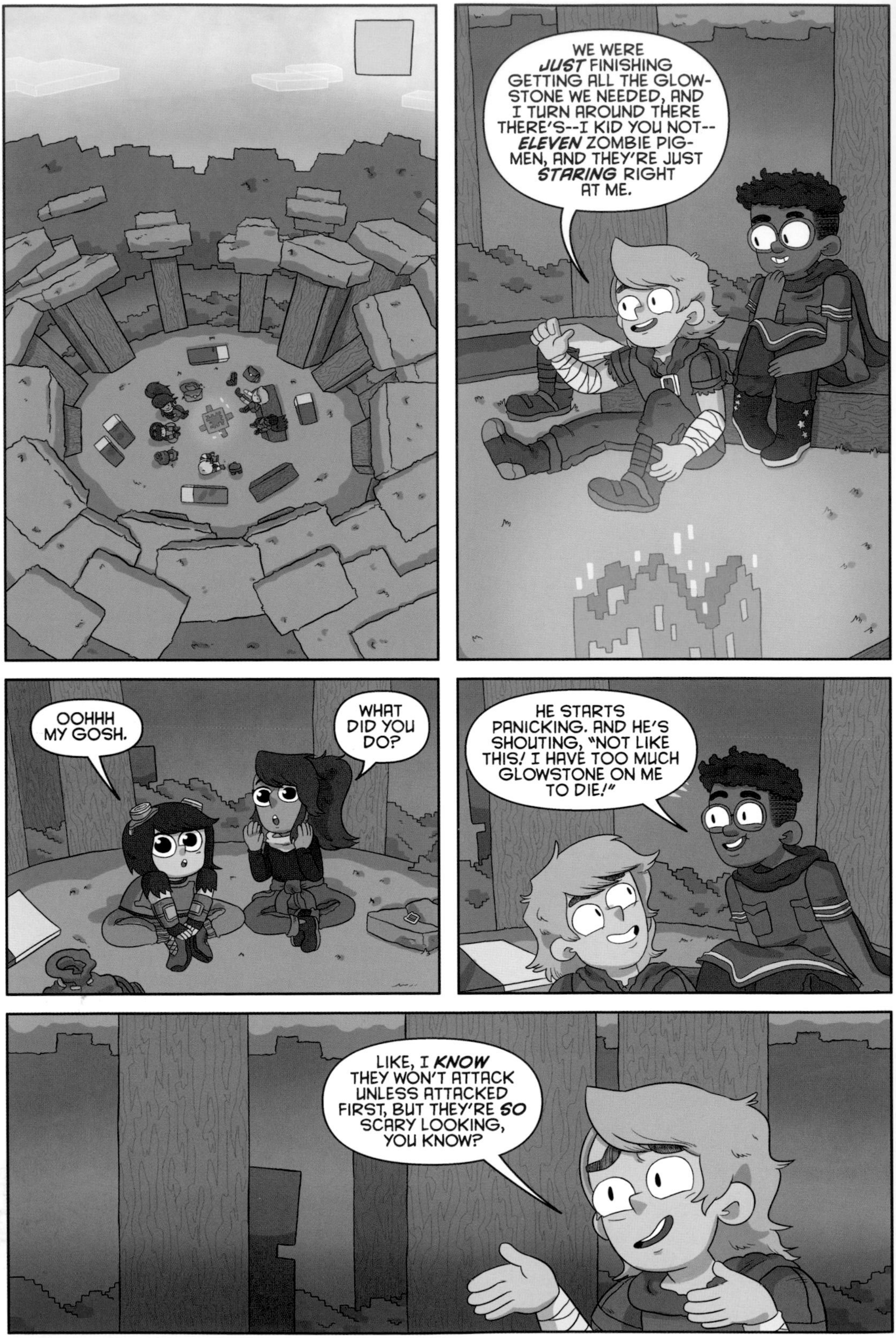
WE WERE JUST FINISHING GETTING ALL THE GLOW-STONE WE NEEDED, AND I TURN AROUND THERE THERE'S--I KID YOU NOT--ELEVEN ZOMBIE PIG-MEN, AND THEY'RE JUST STARING RIGHT AT ME.
OOHHH MY GOSH.
WHAT DID YOU DO?
HE STARTS PANICKING. AND HE'S SHOUTING, "NOT LIKE THIS! I HAVE TOO MUCH GLOWSTONE ON ME TO DIE!"
LIKE, I KNOW THEY WON'T ATTACK UNLESS ATTACKED FIRST, BUT THEY'RE SO SCARY LOOKING, YOU KNOW?

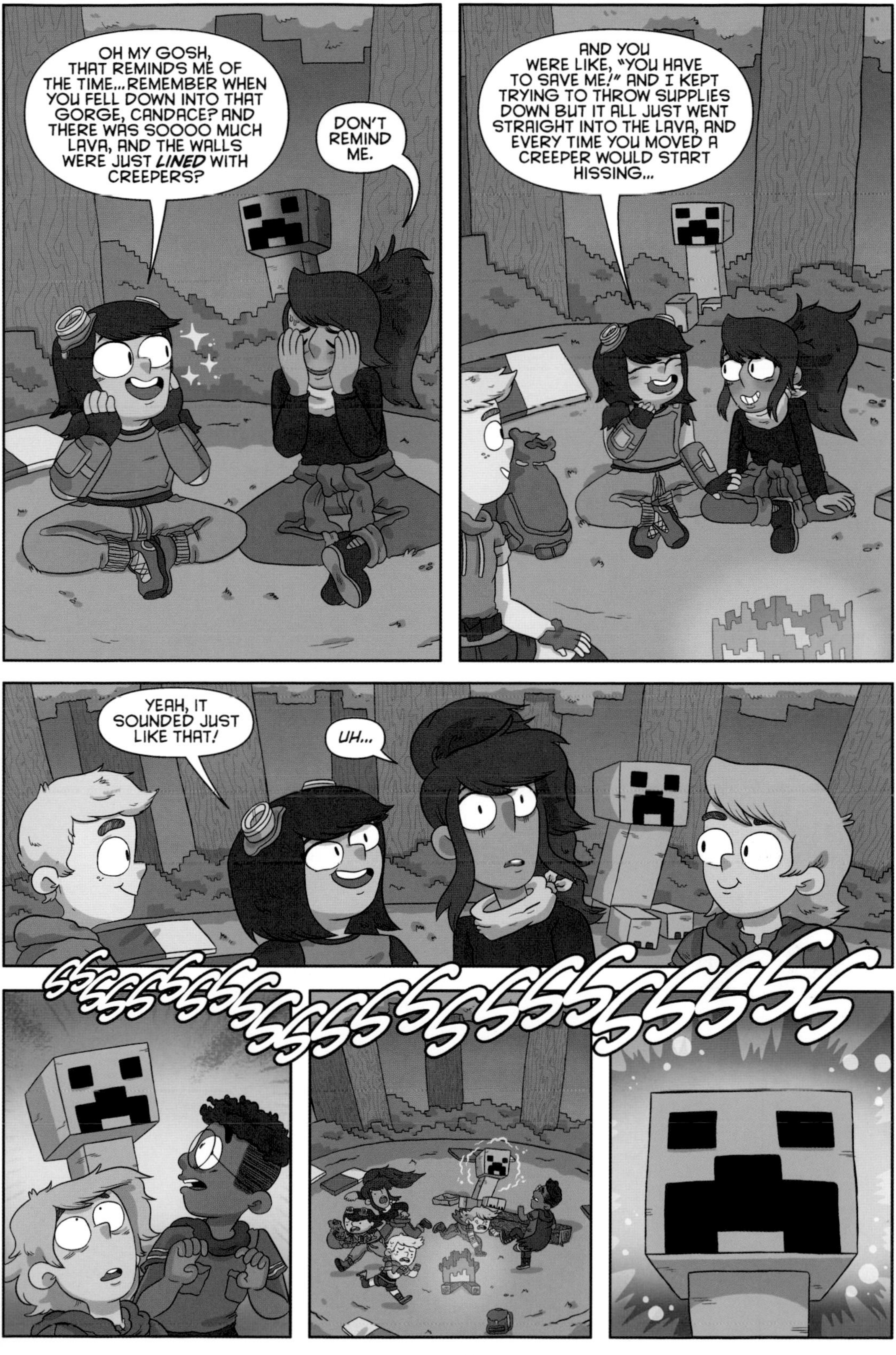
OH MY GOSH, THAT REMINDS ME OF THE TIME... REMEMBER WHEN YOU FELL DOWN INTO THAT GORGE, CANDACE? AND THERE WAS SOOOO MUCH LAVA, AND THE WALLS WERE JUST *LINED* WITH CREEPERS?
DON'T REMIND ME.
AND YOU WERE LIKE, "YOU HAVE TO SAVE ME!" AND I KEPT TRYING TO THROW SUPPLIES DOWN BUT IT ALL JUST WENT STRAIGHT INTO THE LAVA, AND EVERY TIME YOU MOVED A CREEPER WOULD START HISSING...
YEAH, IT SOUNDED JUST LIKE THAT!
UH...
SSSSSSSSSSSSSSSSSSSSSSSSSS

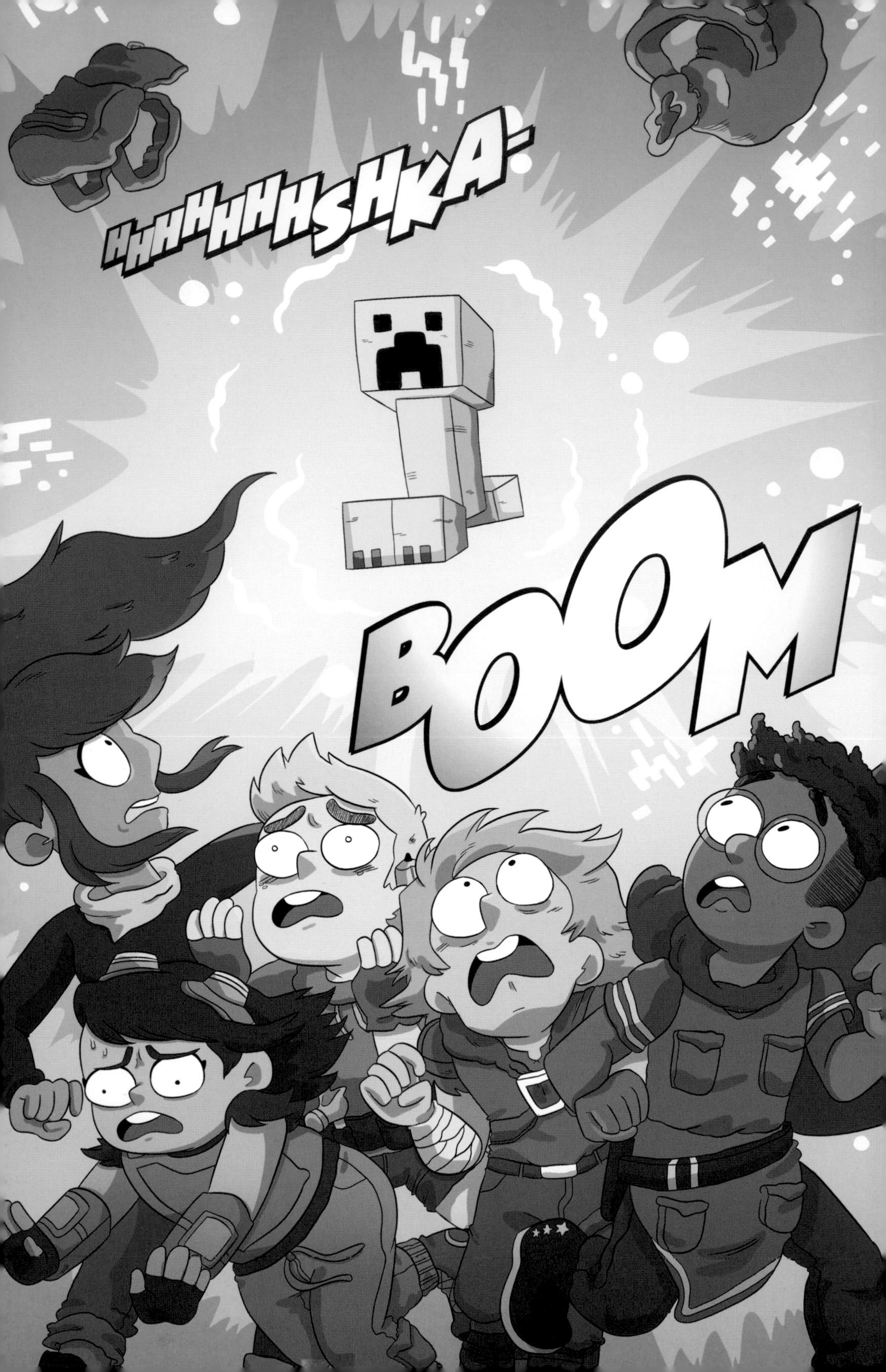
HHHHHHHSHKA-
BOOM

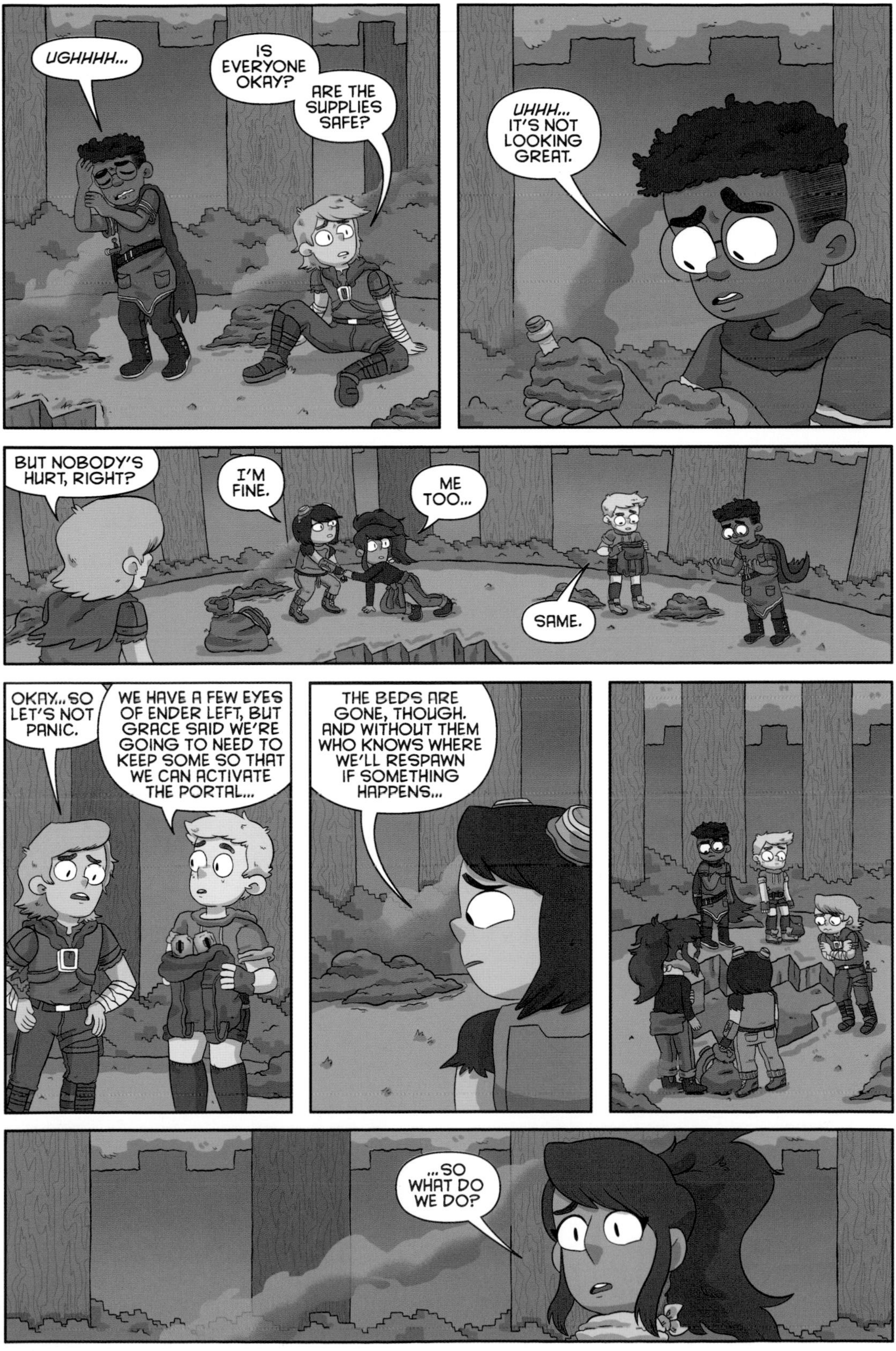

UGHHHH...
IS EVERYONE OKAY?
ARE THE SUPPLIES SAFE?
UHHH... IT'S NOT LOOKING GREAT.
BUT NOBODY'S HURT, RIGHT?
I'M FINE.
ME TOO...
SAME.
OKAY... SO LET'S NOT PANIC.
WE HAVE A FEW EYES OF ENDER LEFT, BUT GRACE SAID WE'RE GOING TO NEED TO KEEP SOME SO THAT WE CAN ACTIVATE THE PORTAL...
THE BEDS ARE GONE, THOUGH. AND WITHOUT THEM WHO KNOWS WHERE WE'LL RESPAWN IF SOMETHING HAPPENS...
...SO WHAT DO WE DO?

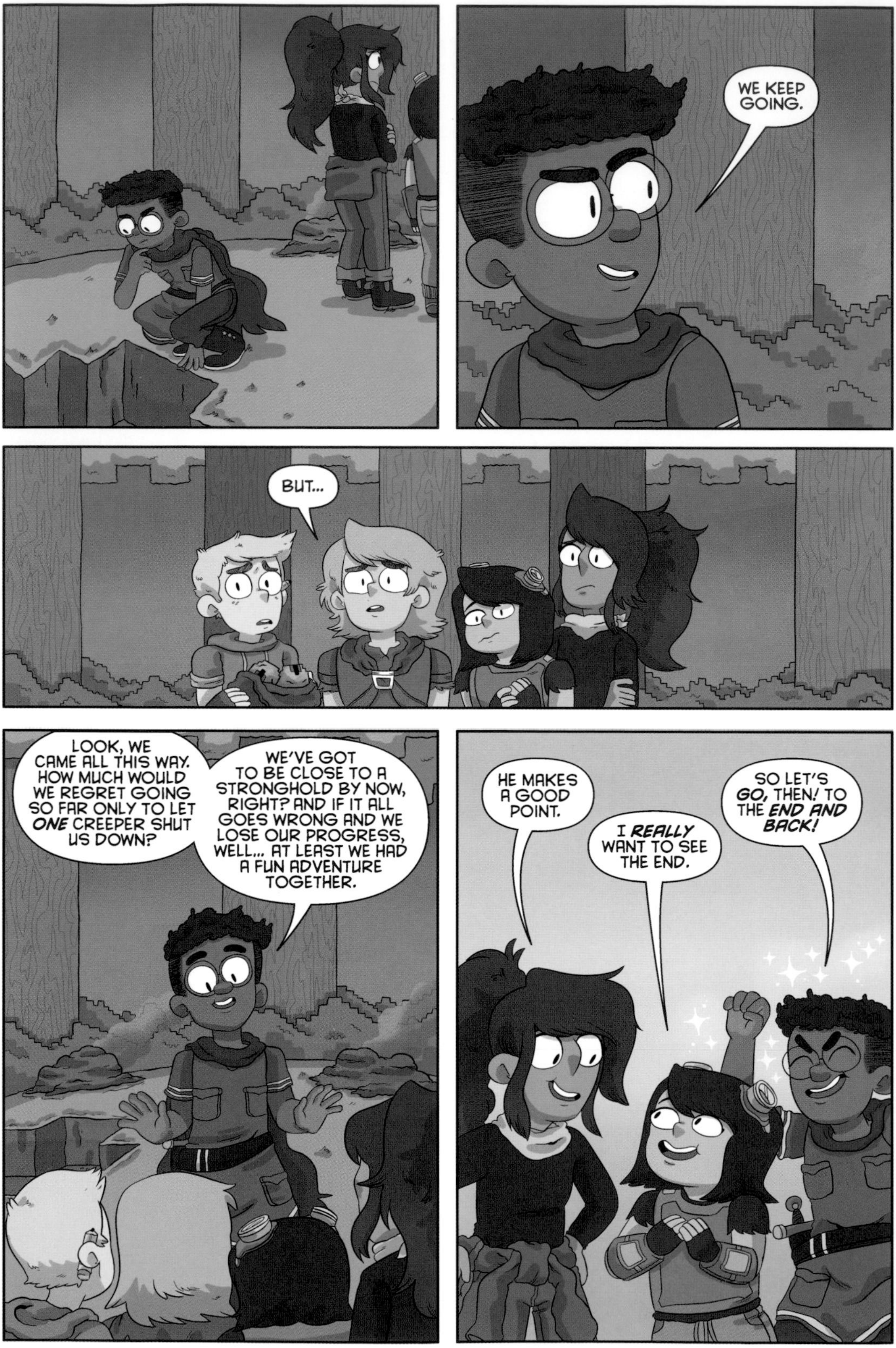

WE KEEP GOING.
BUT...
LOOK, WE CAME ALL THIS WAY. HOW MUCH WOULD WE REGRET GOING SO FAR ONLY TO LET *ONE* CREEPER SHUT US DOWN?
WE'VE GOT TO BE CLOSE TO A STRONGHOLD BY NOW, RIGHT? AND IF IT ALL GOES WRONG AND WE LOSE OUR PROGRESS, WELL... AT LEAST WE HAD A FUN ADVENTURE TOGETHER.
HE MAKES A GOOD POINT.
I *REALLY* WANT TO SEE THE END.
SO LET'S *GO,* THEN! TO THE *END AND BACK!*

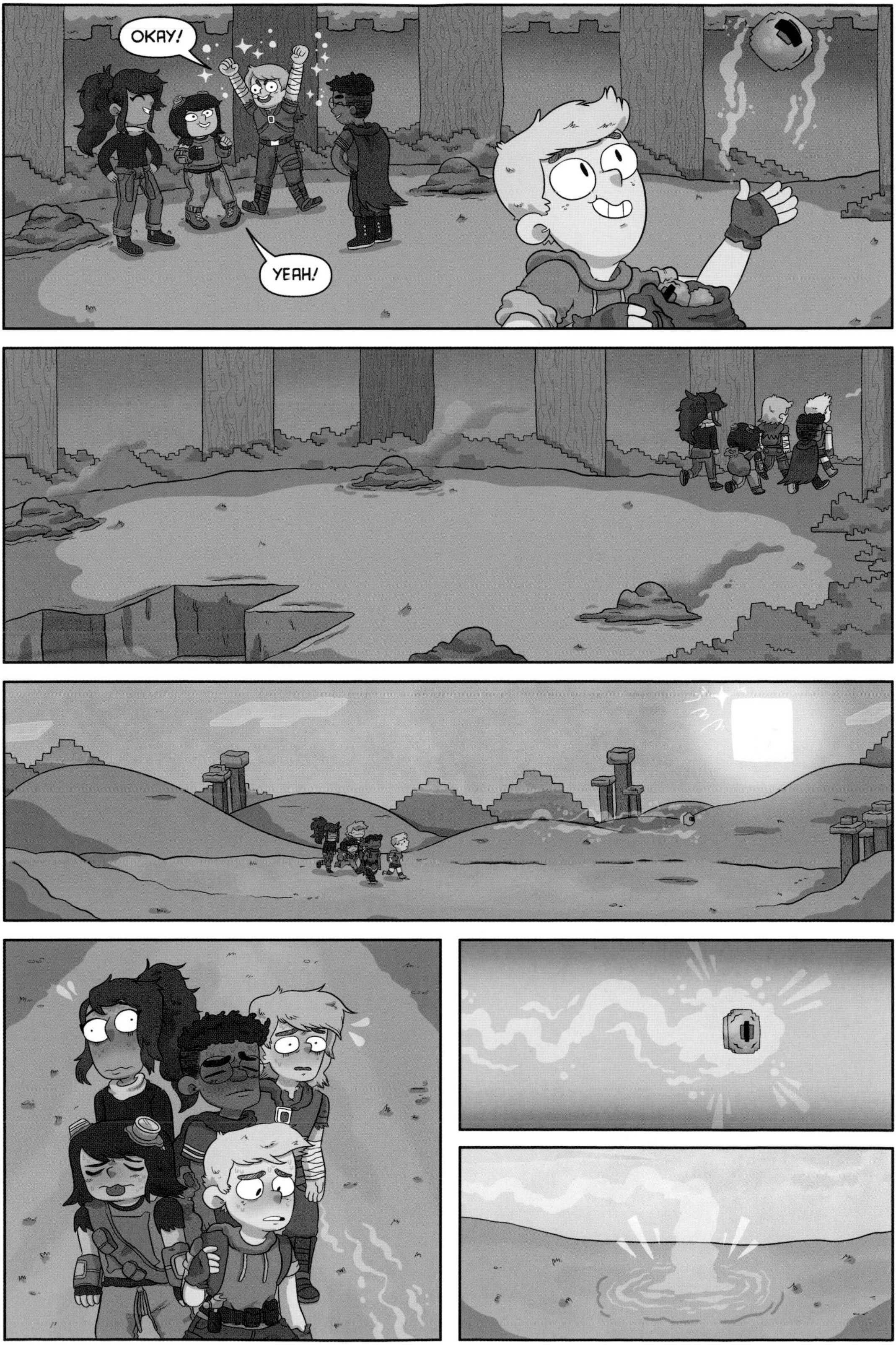
OKAY!
YEAH!

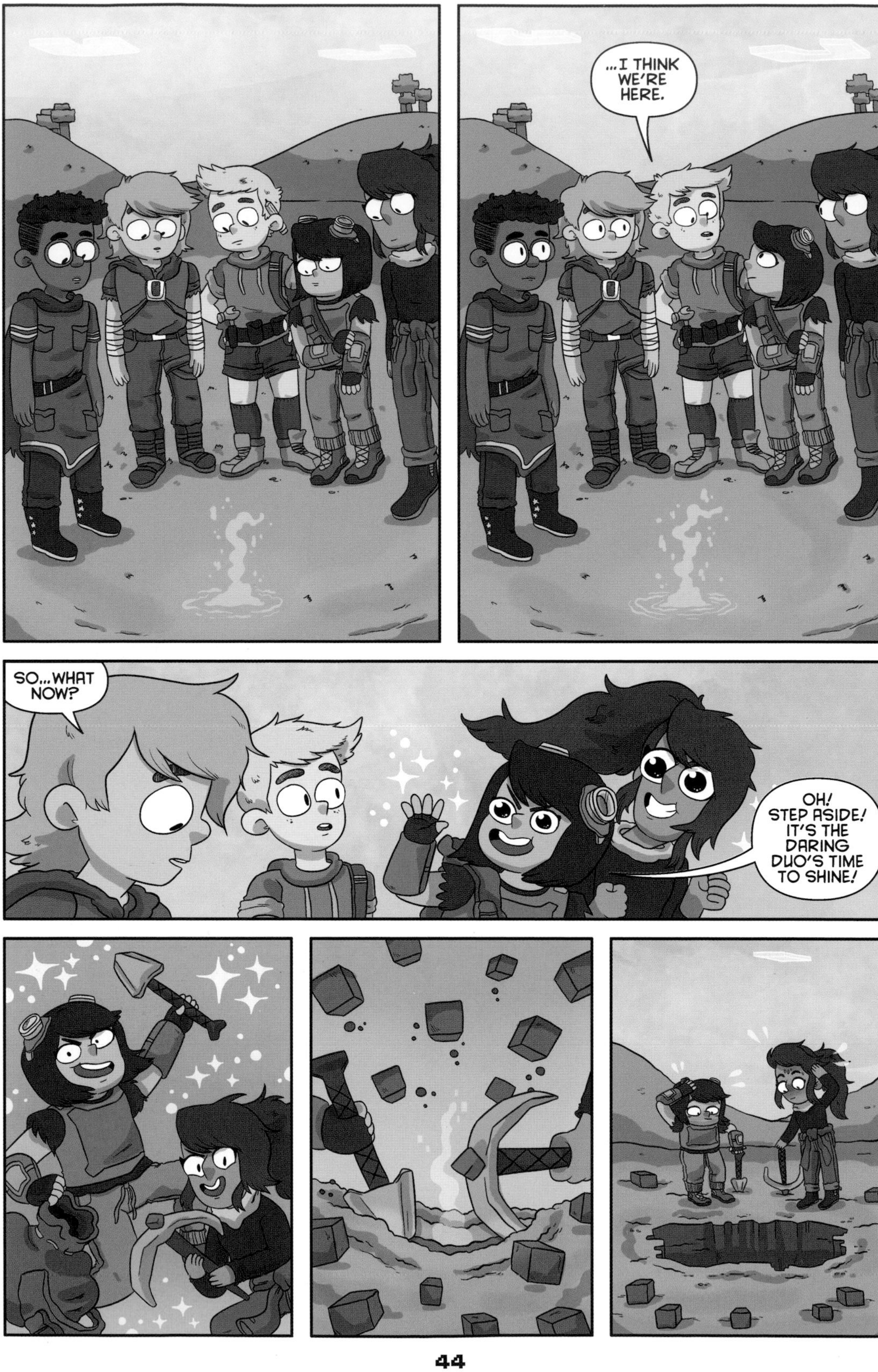
...I THINK WE'RE HERE.
SO...WHAT NOW?
OH! STEP ASIDE! IT'S THE DARING DUO'S TIME TO SHINE!

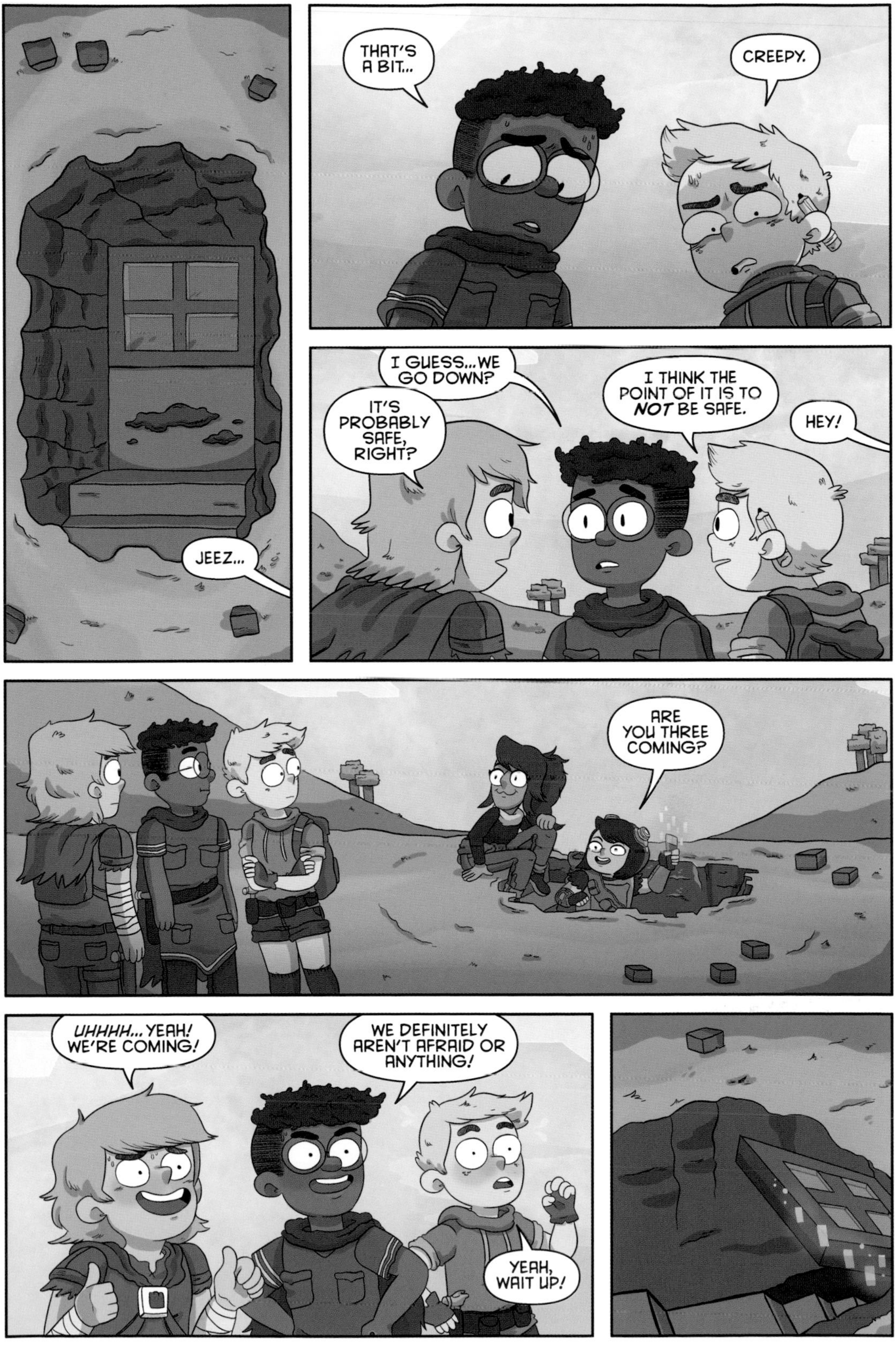
JEEZ...
THAT'S A BIT...
CREEPY.
I GUESS...WE GO DOWN?
IT'S PROBABLY SAFE, RIGHT?
I THINK THE POINT OF IT IS TO *NOT* BE SAFE.
HEY!
ARE YOU THREE COMING?
UHHHH... YEAH! WE'RE COMING!
WE DEFINITELY AREN'T AFRAID OR ANYTHING!
YEAH, WAIT UP!

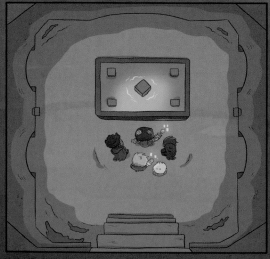

WHERE ARE WE...?

THIS IS THE ENTRY OF A STRONGHOLD...

MAKE SURE YOU DON'T BREAK ANYTHING. THE WALLS ARE SUPPOSEDLY LINED WITH MOB EGGS--

--IF WE DISTURB ANYTHING WE'RE GOING TO BE IN A *LOT* OF TROUBLE.

WHICH WAY SHOULD WE GO?

HEY.

THERE'S A LIGHT DOWN THERE.

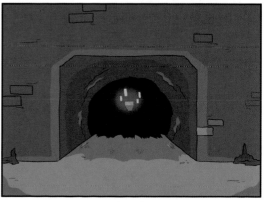

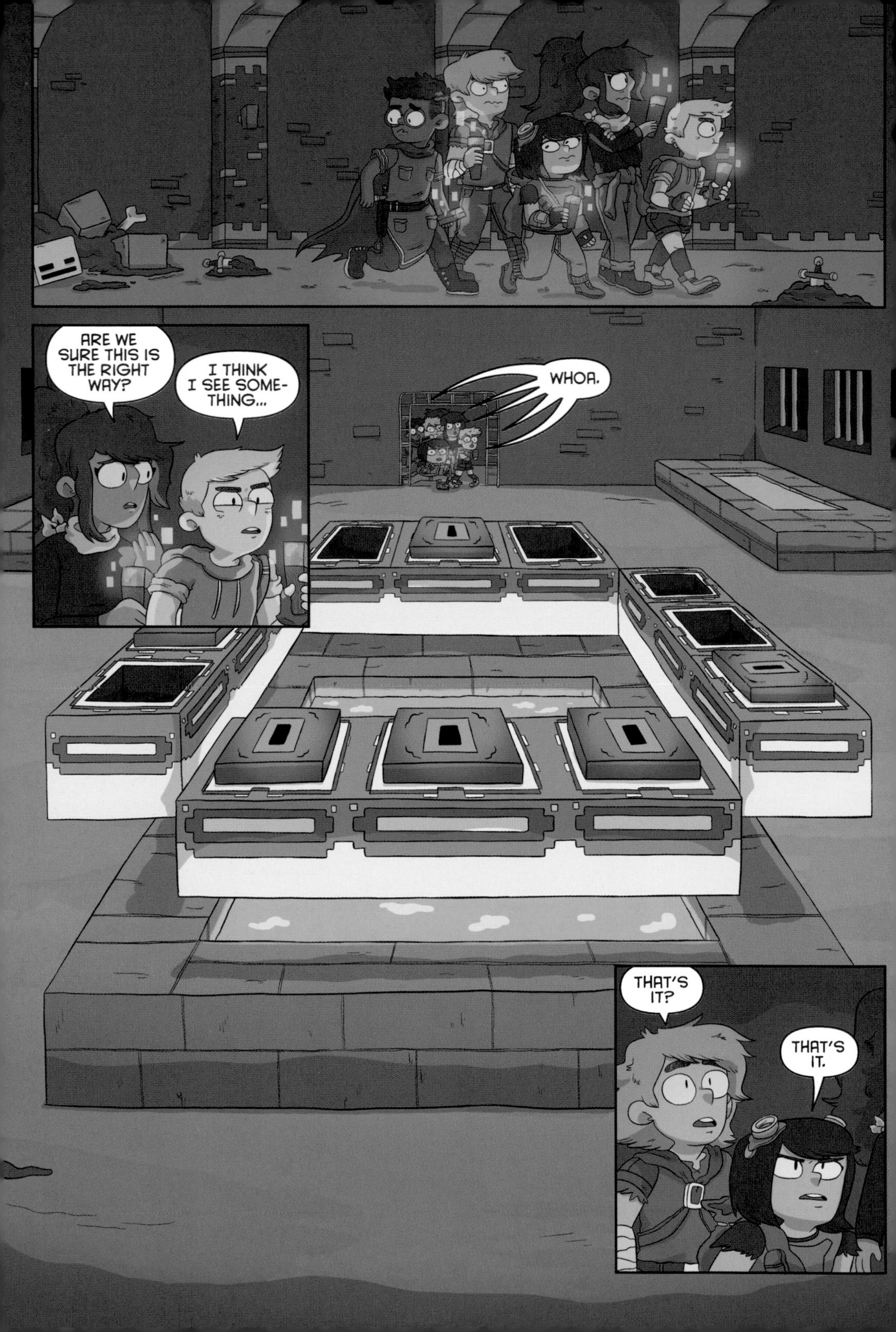
ARE WE SURE THIS IS THE RIGHT WAY?
I THINK I SEE SOME-THING...
WHOA.
THAT'S IT?
THAT'S IT.

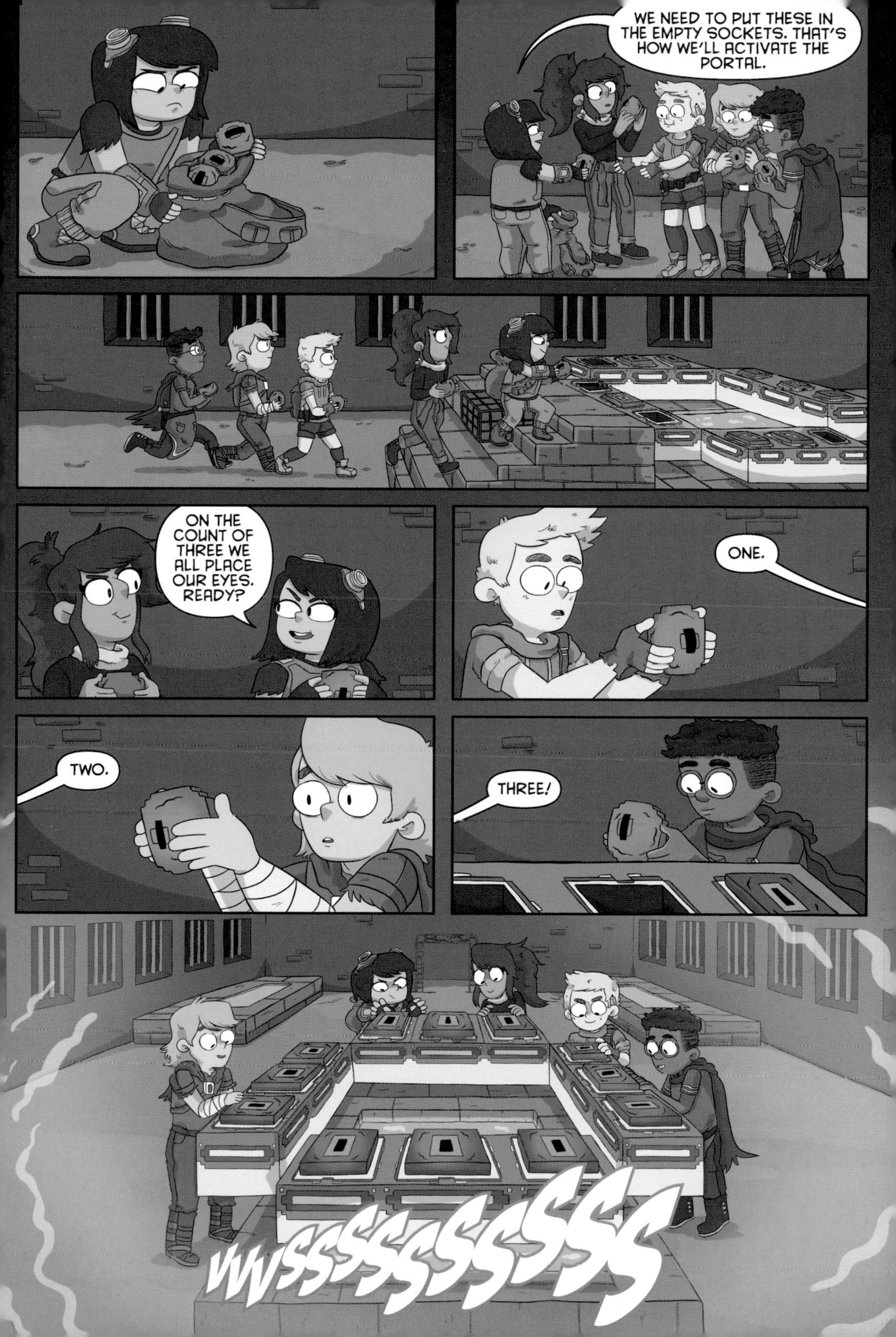
WE NEED TO PUT THESE IN THE EMPTY SOCKETS. THAT'S HOW WE'LL ACTIVATE THE PORTAL.
ON THE COUNT OF THREE WE ALL PLACE OUR EYES. READY?
ONE.
TWO.
THREE!
VVVSSSSSSSSSSS

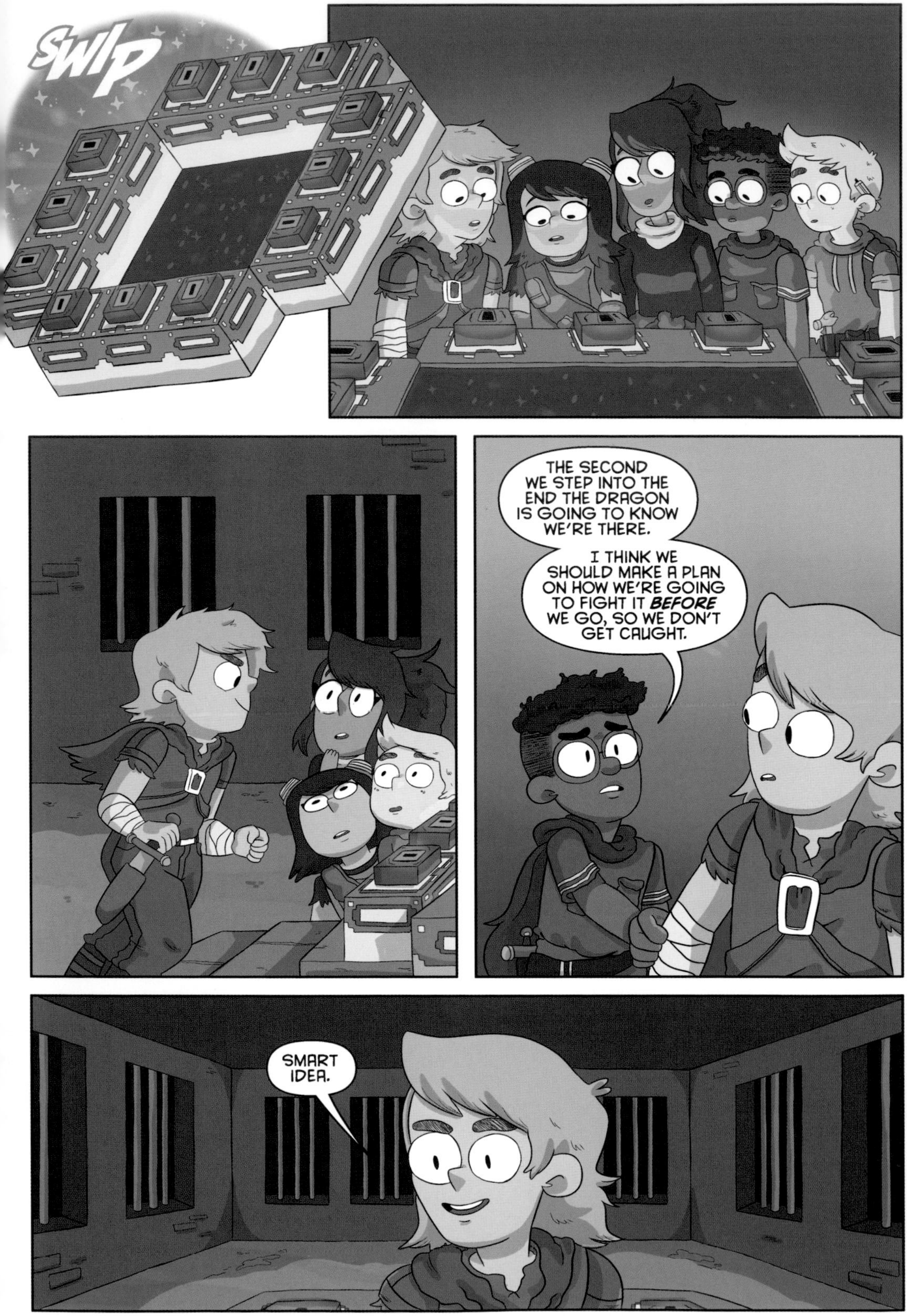
SWIP
THE SECOND WE STEP INTO THE END THE DRAGON IS GOING TO KNOW WE'RE THERE.
I THINK WE SHOULD MAKE A PLAN ON HOW WE'RE GOING TO FIGHT IT *BEFORE* WE GO, SO WE DON'T GET CAUGHT.
SMART IDEA.

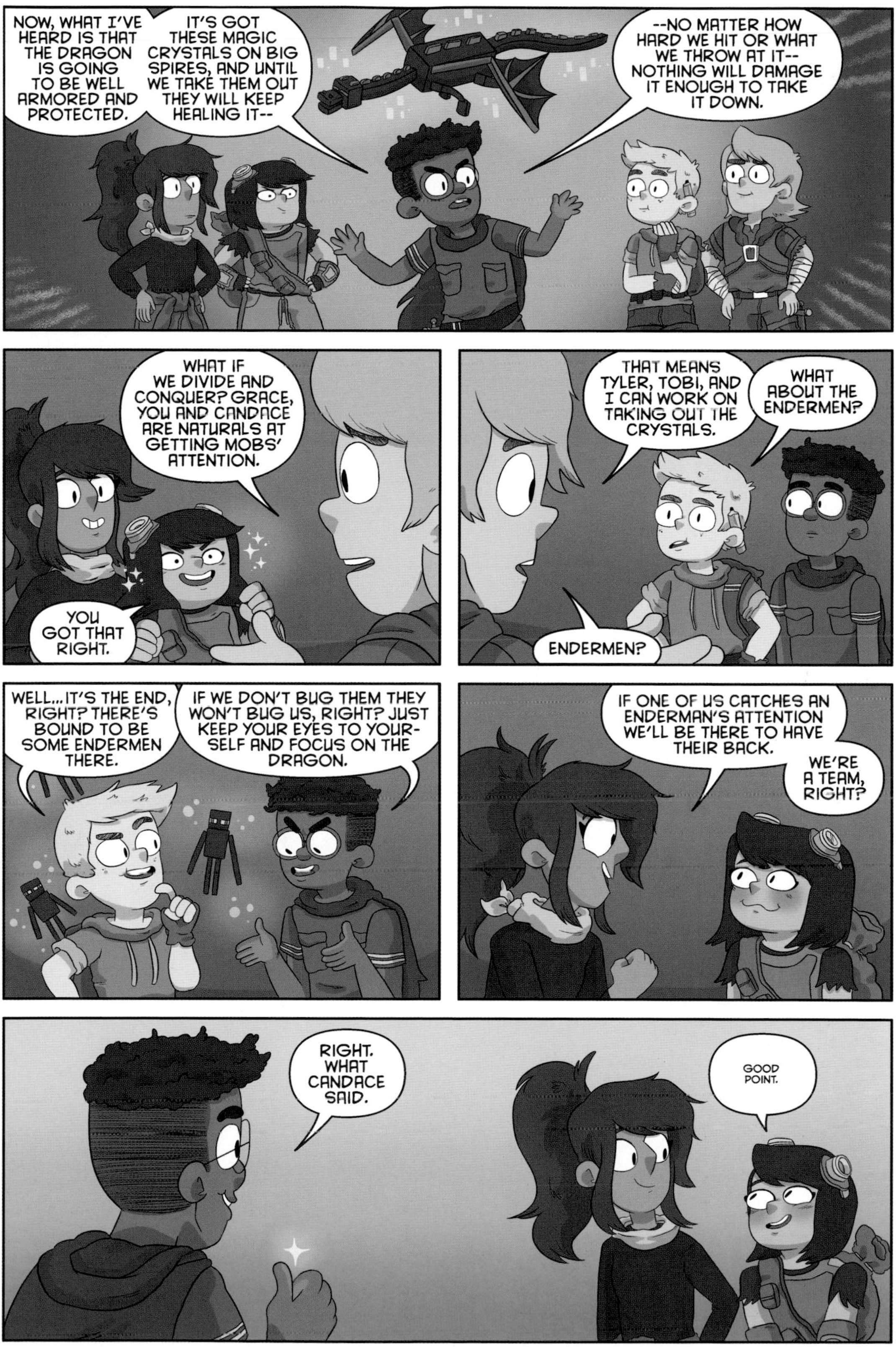
NOW, WHAT I'VE HEARD IS THAT THE DRAGON IS GOING TO BE WELL ARMORED AND PROTECTED.
IT'S GOT THESE MAGIC CRYSTALS ON BIG SPIRES, AND UNTIL WE TAKE THEM OUT THEY WILL KEEP HEALING IT--
--NO MATTER HOW HARD WE HIT OR WHAT WE THROW AT IT-- NOTHING WILL DAMAGE IT ENOUGH TO TAKE IT DOWN.
WHAT IF WE DIVIDE AND CONQUER? GRACE, YOU AND CANDACE ARE NATURALS AT GETTING MOBS' ATTENTION.
YOU GOT THAT RIGHT.
THAT MEANS TYLER, TOBI, AND I CAN WORK ON TAKING OUT THE CRYSTALS.
WHAT ABOUT THE ENDERMEN?
ENDERMEN?
WELL... IT'S THE END, RIGHT? THERE'S BOUND TO BE SOME ENDERMEN THERE.
IF WE DON'T BUG THEM THEY WON'T BUG US, RIGHT? JUST KEEP YOUR EYES TO YOURSELF AND FOCUS ON THE DRAGON.
IF ONE OF US CATCHES AN ENDERMAN'S ATTENTION WE'LL BE THERE TO HAVE THEIR BACK.
WE'RE A TEAM, RIGHT?
RIGHT. WHAT CANDACE SAID.
GOOD POINT.

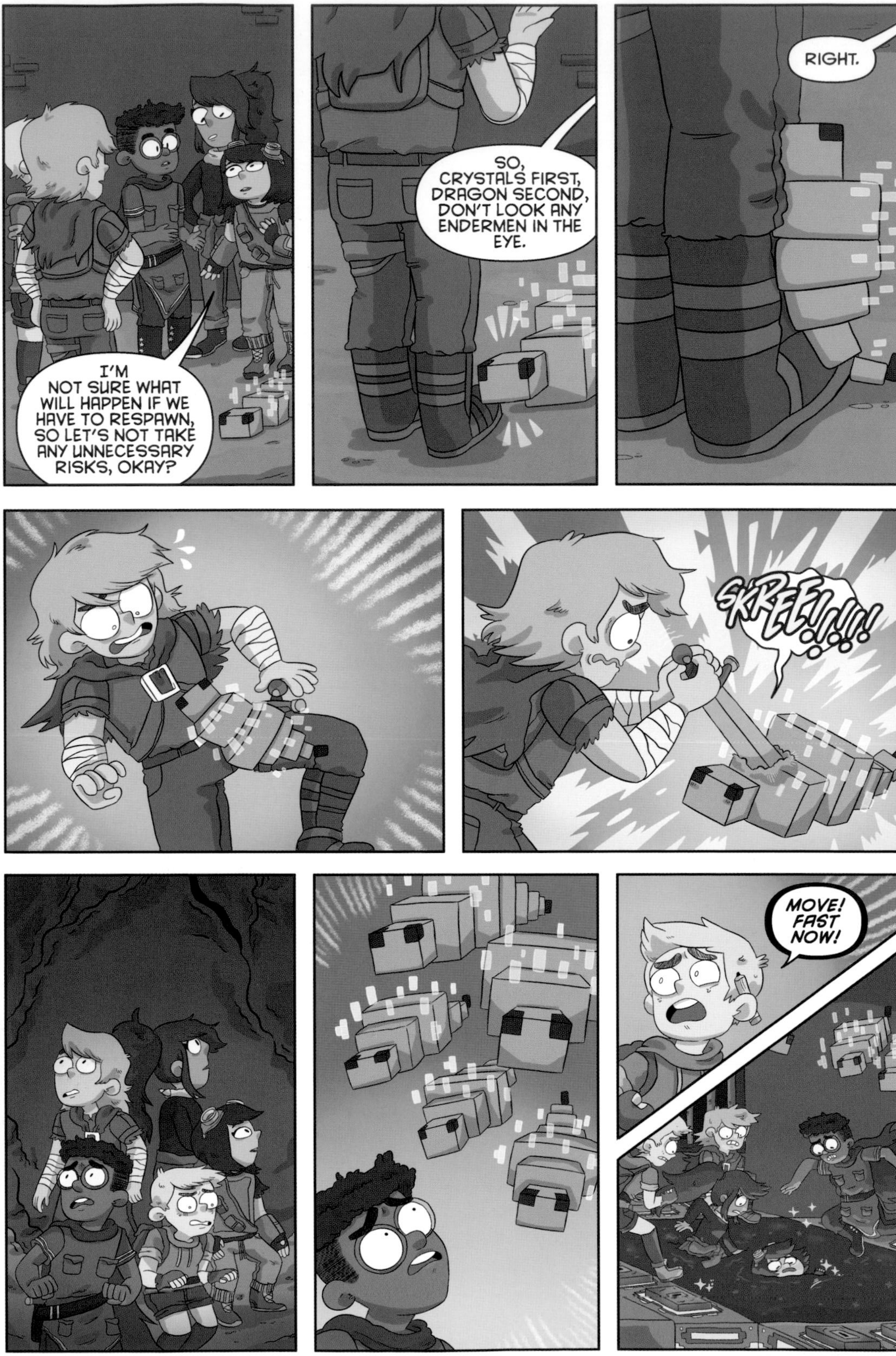
I'M NOT SURE WHAT WILL HAPPEN IF WE HAVE TO RESPAWN, SO LET'S NOT TAKE ANY UNNECESSARY RISKS, OKAY?
SO, CRYSTALS FIRST, DRAGON SECOND, DON'T LOOK ANY ENDERMEN IN THE EYE.
RIGHT.
SKREEE!!!!!!
MOVE! FAST NOW!

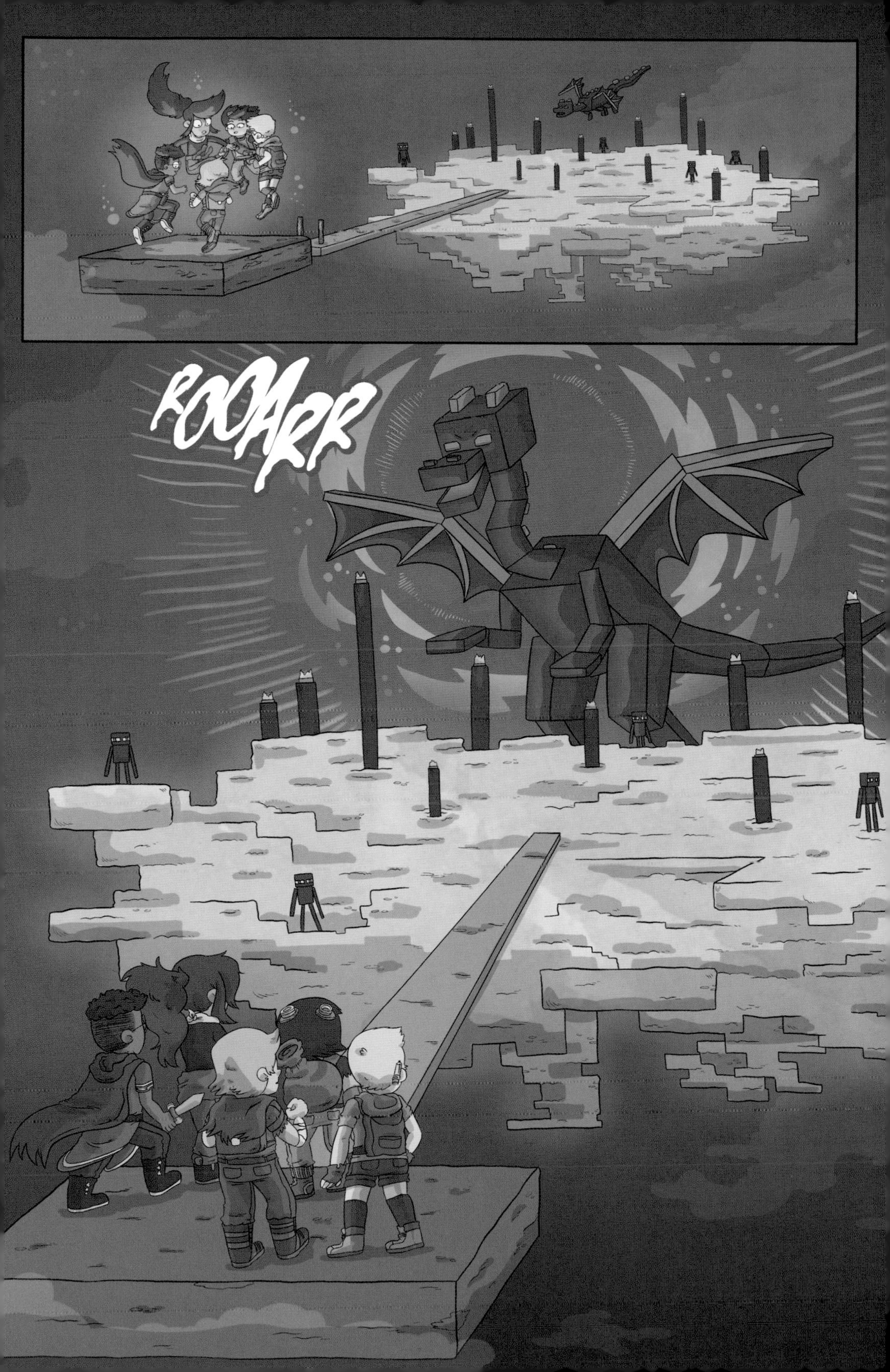
ROOARR

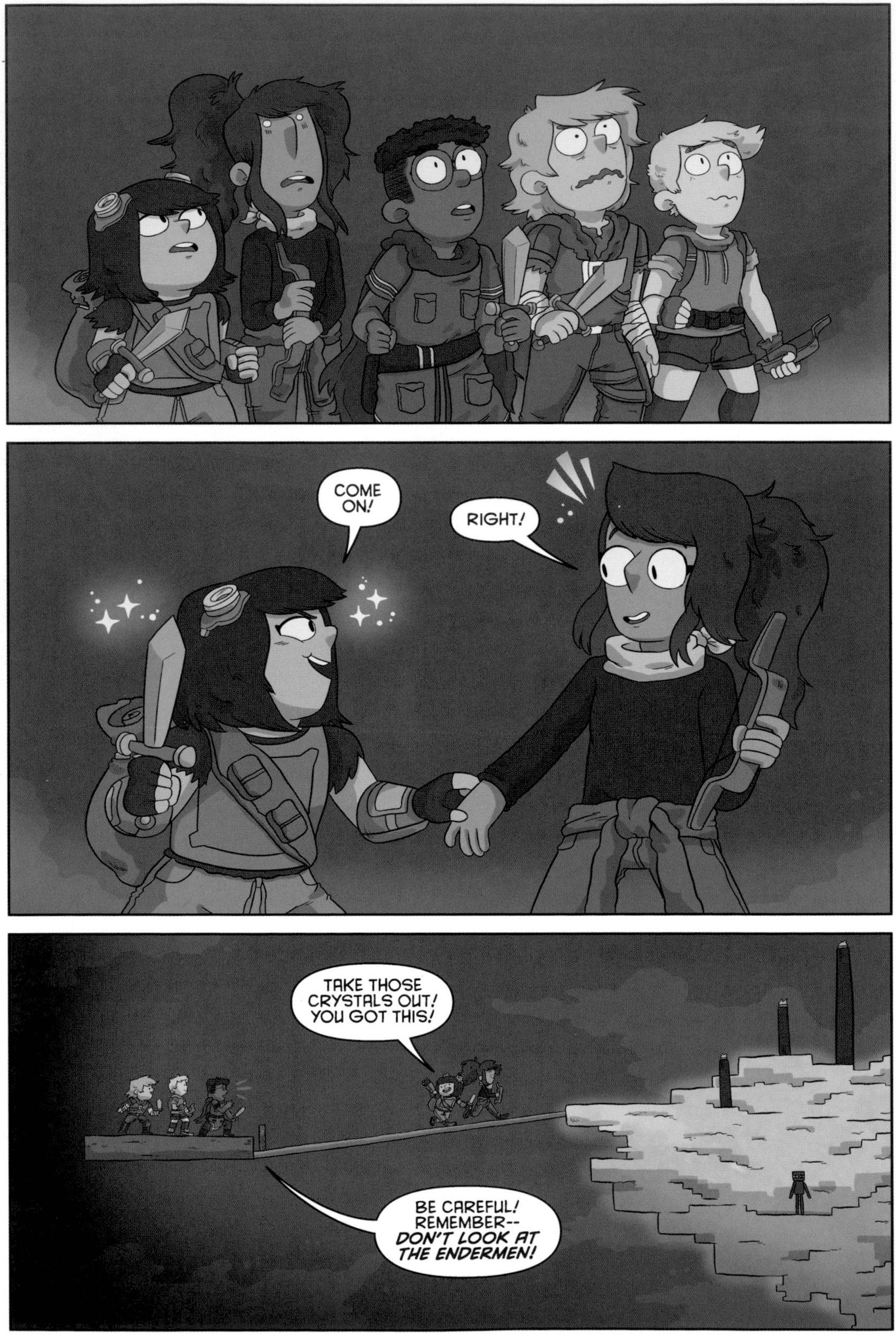
COME ON!
RIGHT!
TAKE THOSE CRYSTALS OUT! YOU GOT THIS!
BE CAREFUL! REMEMBER-- *DON'T LOOK AT THE ENDERMEN!*

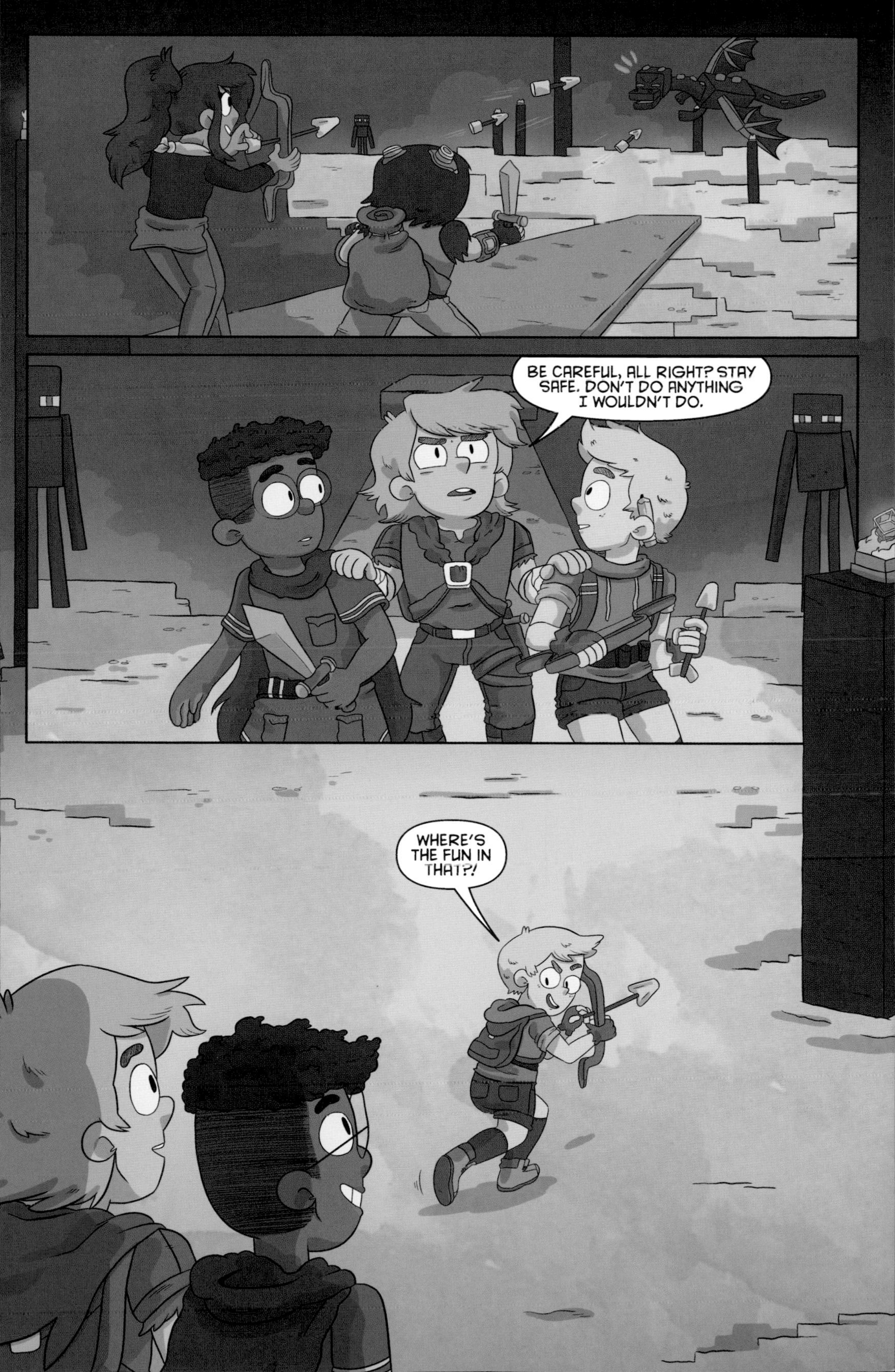
BE CAREFUL, ALL RIGHT? STAY SAFE. DON'T DO ANYTHING I WOULDN'T DO.
WHERE'S THE FUN IN THAT?!

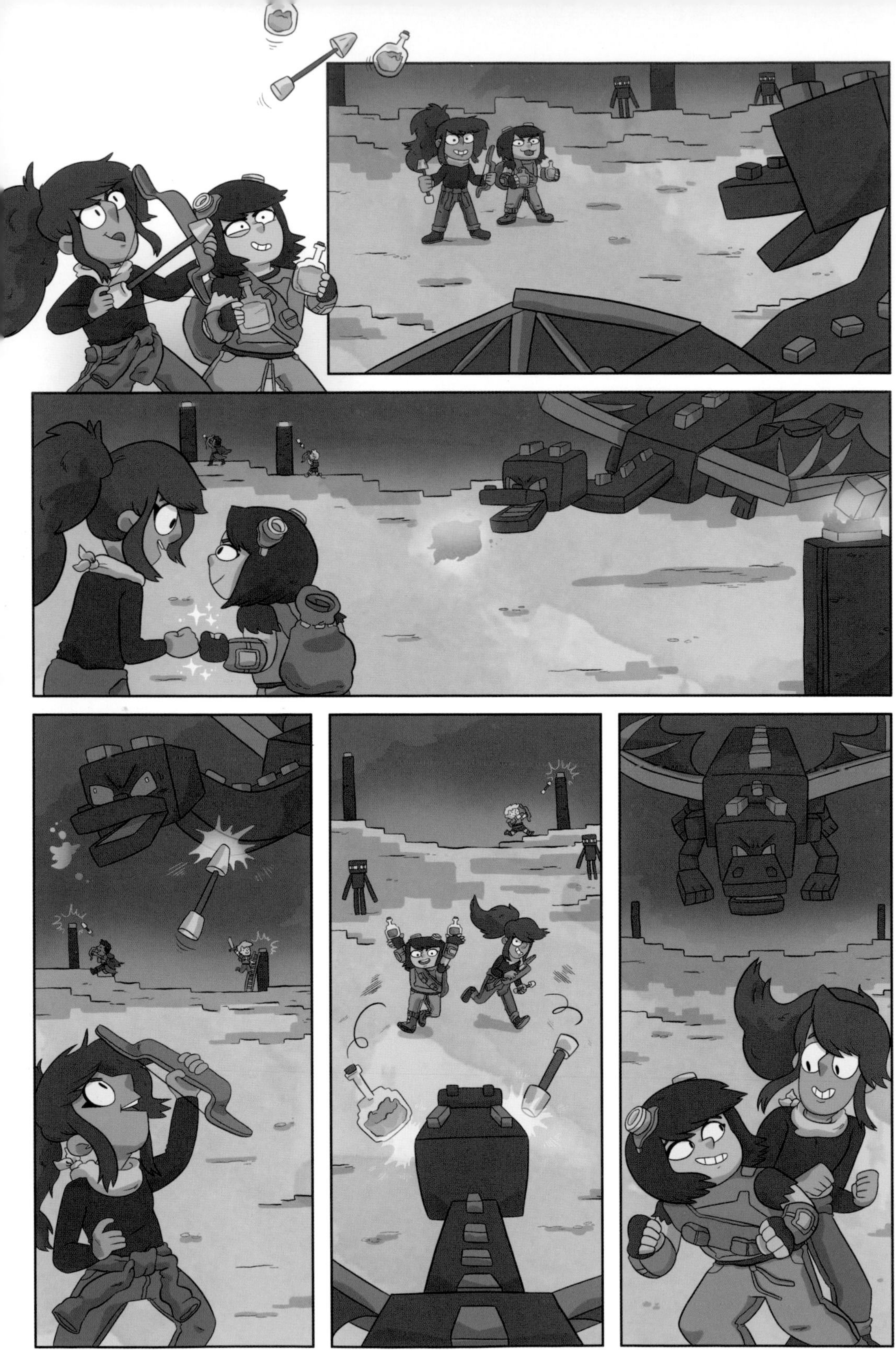

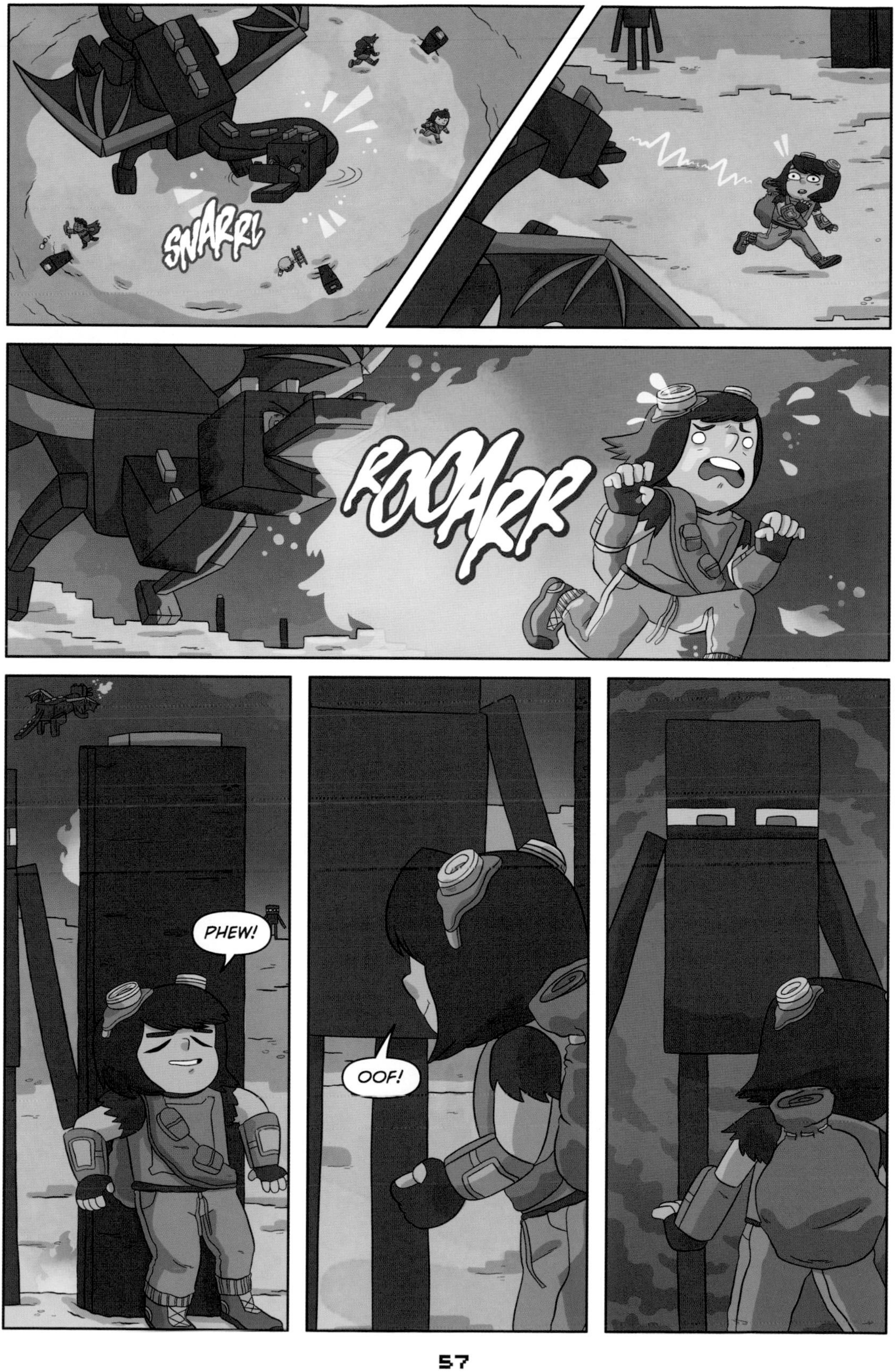
SNARRL
ROOARR
PHEW!
OOF!

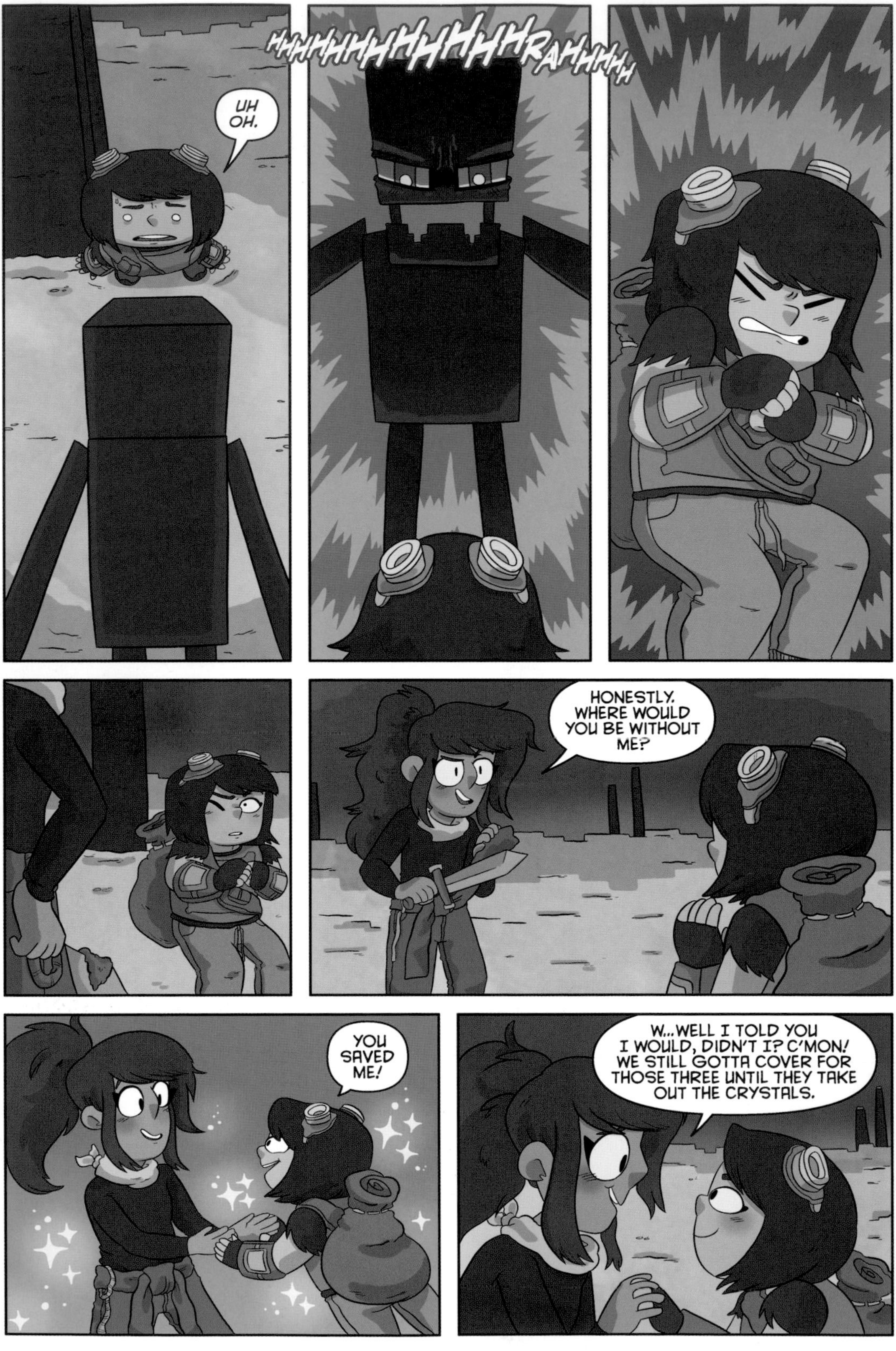
UH OH.
HHHHHHHHHHHHHHRAHHHHH
HONESTLY. WHERE WOULD YOU BE WITHOUT ME?
YOU SAVED ME!
W...WELL I TOLD YOU I WOULD, DIDN'T I? C'MON! WE STILL GOTTA COVER FOR THOSE THREE UNTIL THEY TAKE OUT THE CRYSTALS.

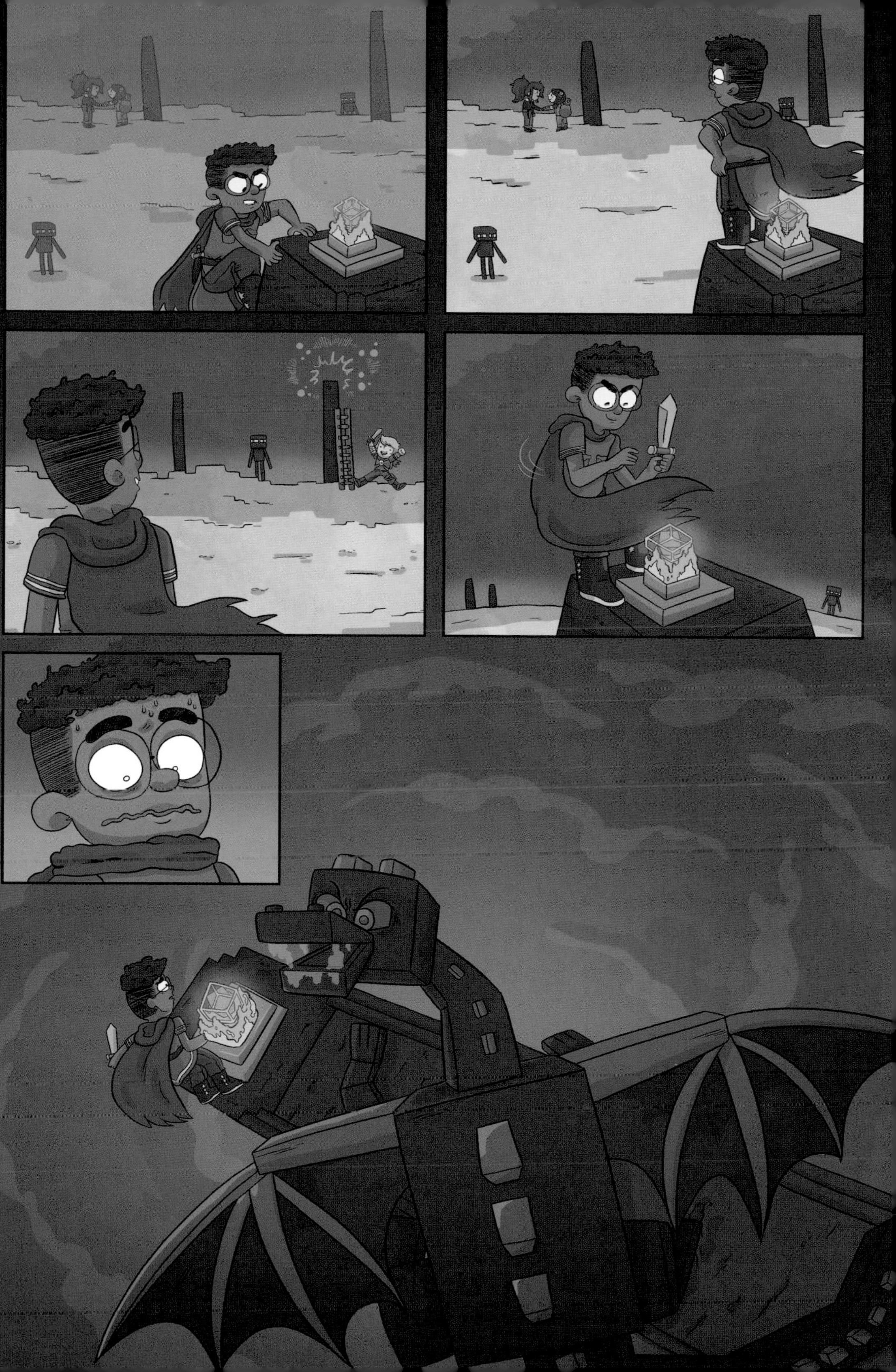

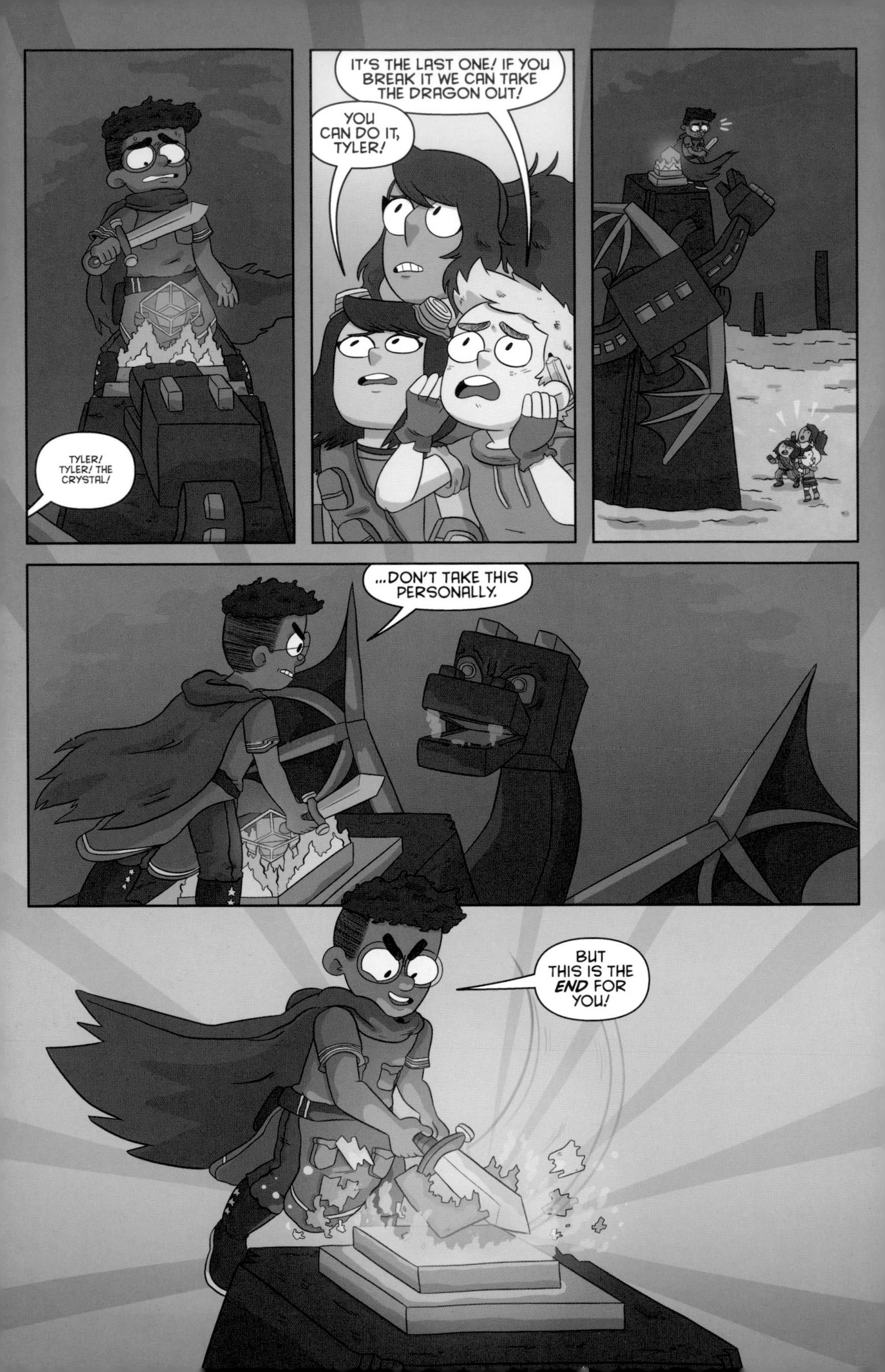
TYLER! TYLER! THE CRYSTAL!
IT'S THE LAST ONE! IF YOU BREAK IT WE CAN TAKE THE DRAGON OUT!
YOU CAN DO IT, TYLER!
...DON'T TAKE THIS PERSONALLY.
BUT THIS IS THE END FOR YOU!

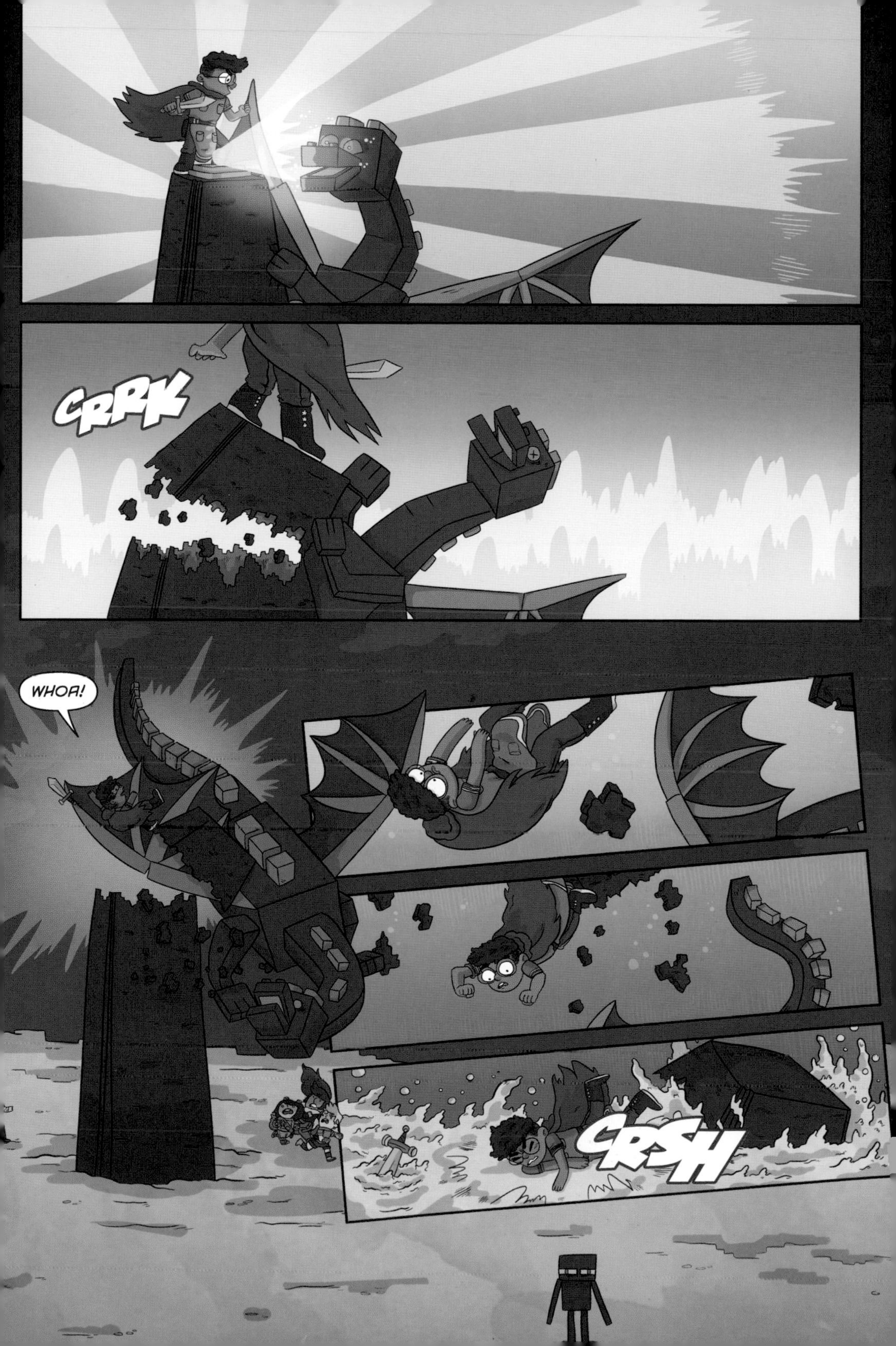
CRRK
WHOA!
CRSH

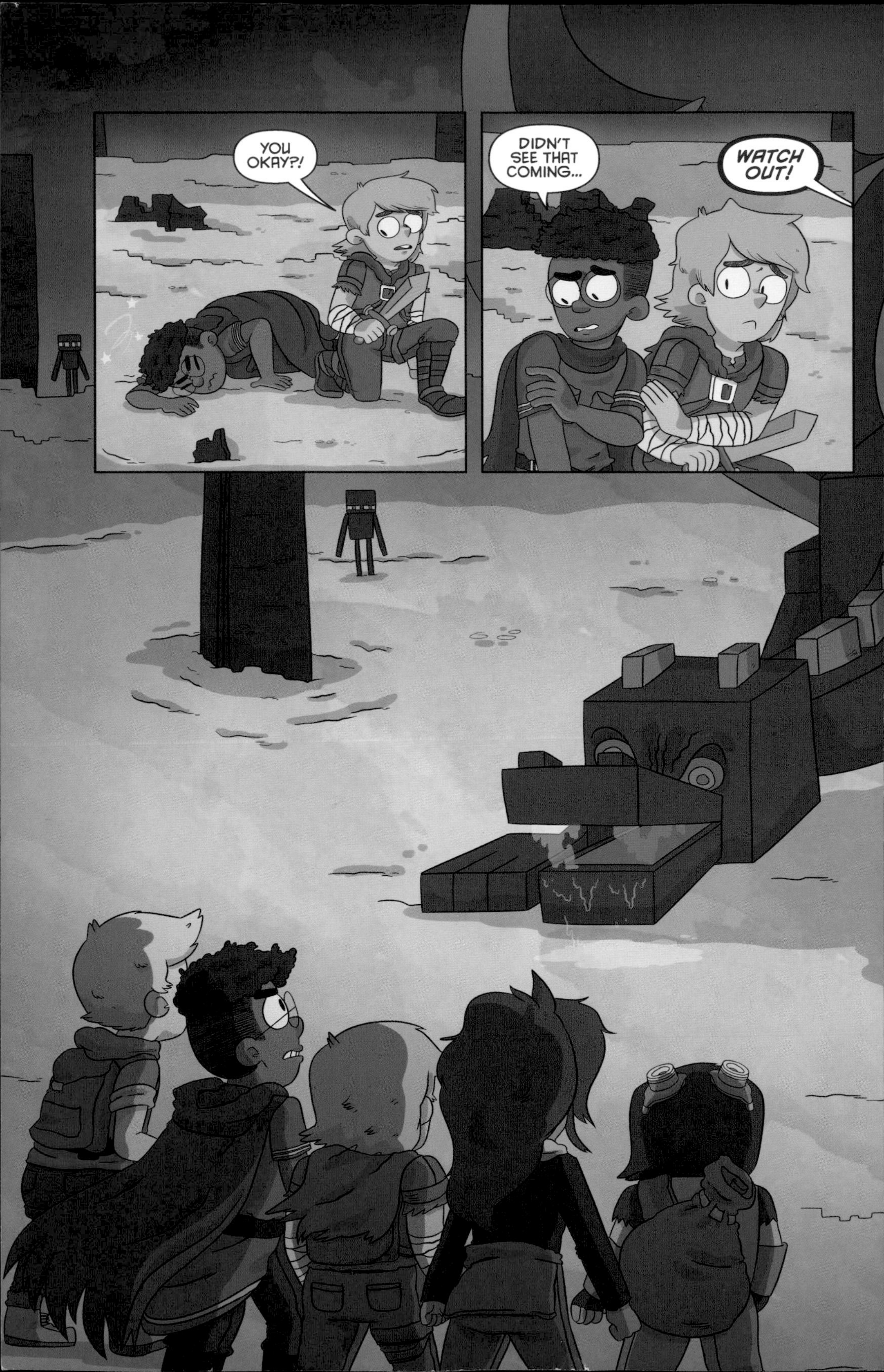
YOU OKAY?!
DIDN'T SEE THAT COMING...
WATCH OUT!

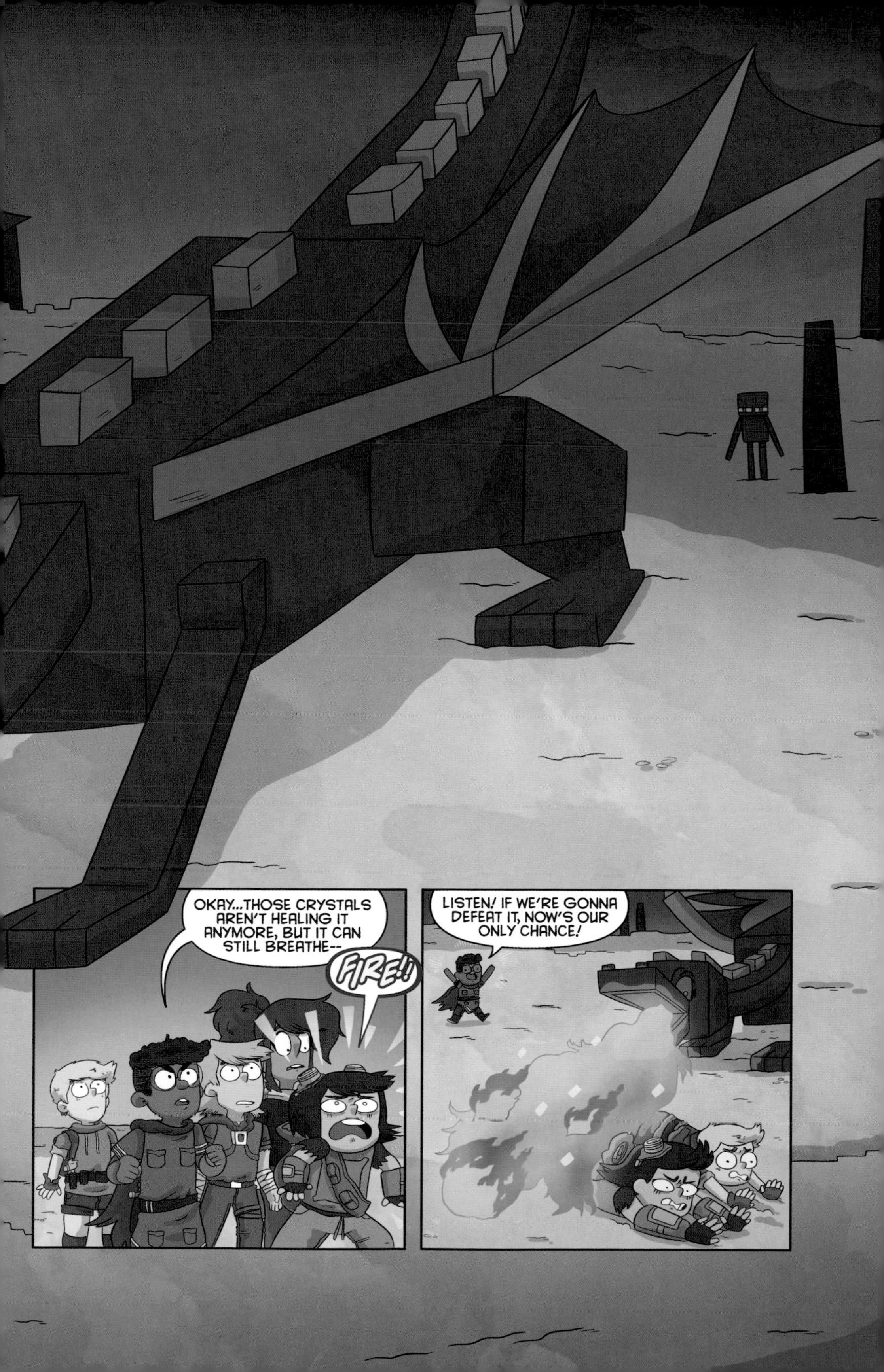
OKAY...THOSE CRYSTALS AREN'T HEALING IT ANYMORE, BUT IT CAN STILL BREATHE--
FIRE!!
LISTEN! IF WE'RE GONNA DEFEAT IT, NOW'S OUR ONLY CHANCE!

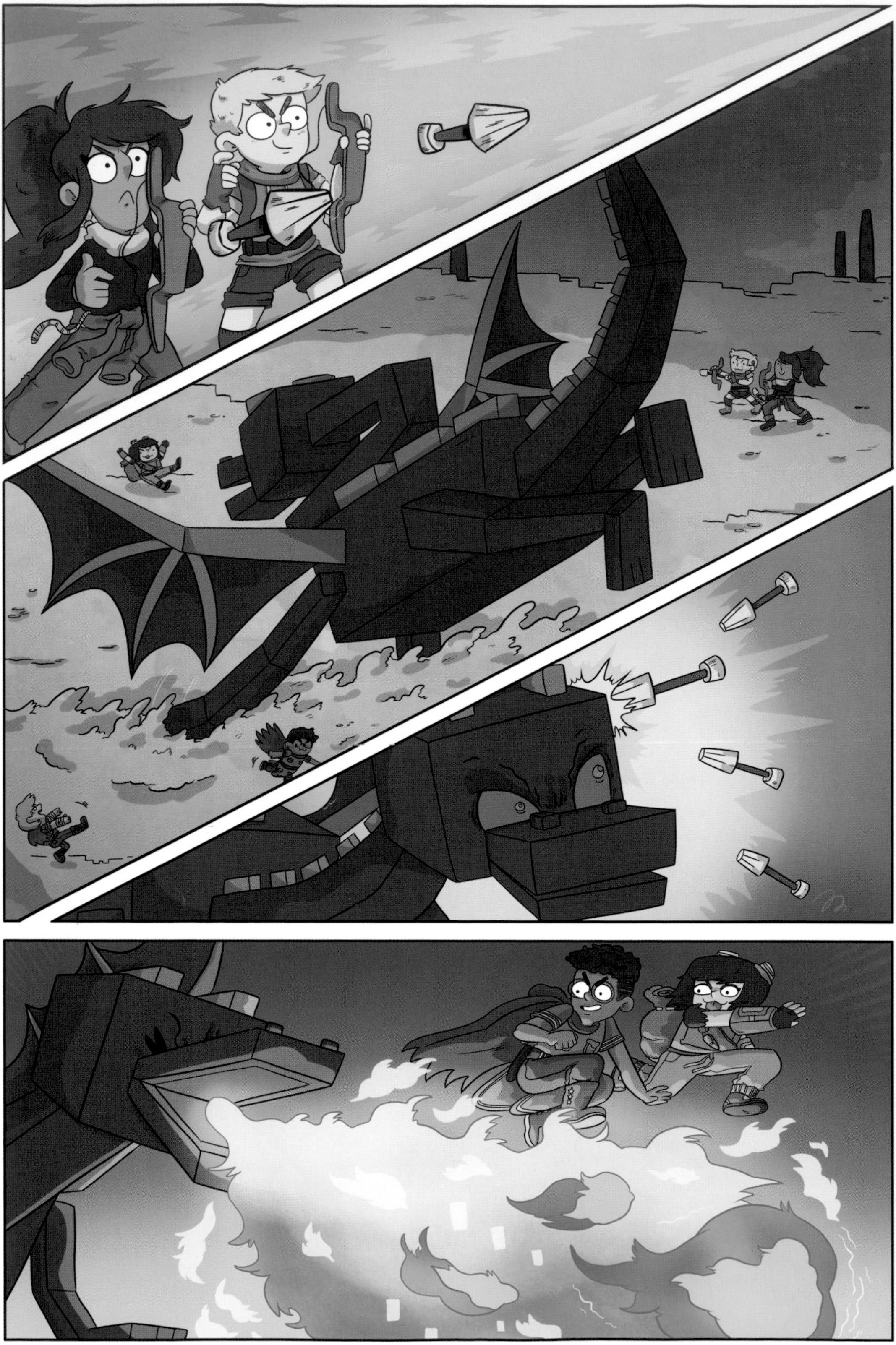

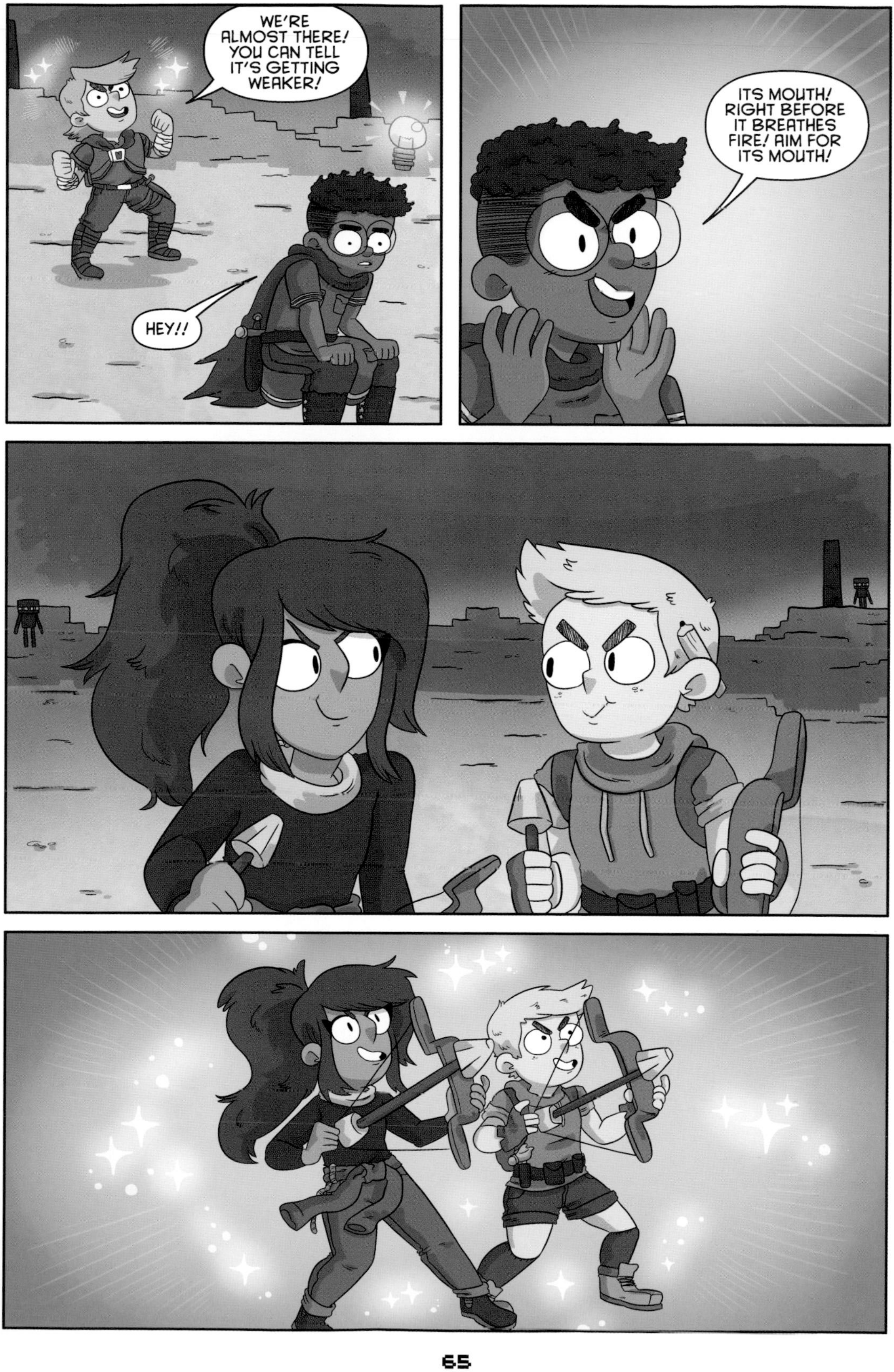
WE'RE ALMOST THERE! YOU CAN TELL IT'S GETTING WEAKER!
HEY!!
ITS MOUTH! RIGHT BEFORE IT BREATHES FIRE! AIM FOR ITS MOUTH!

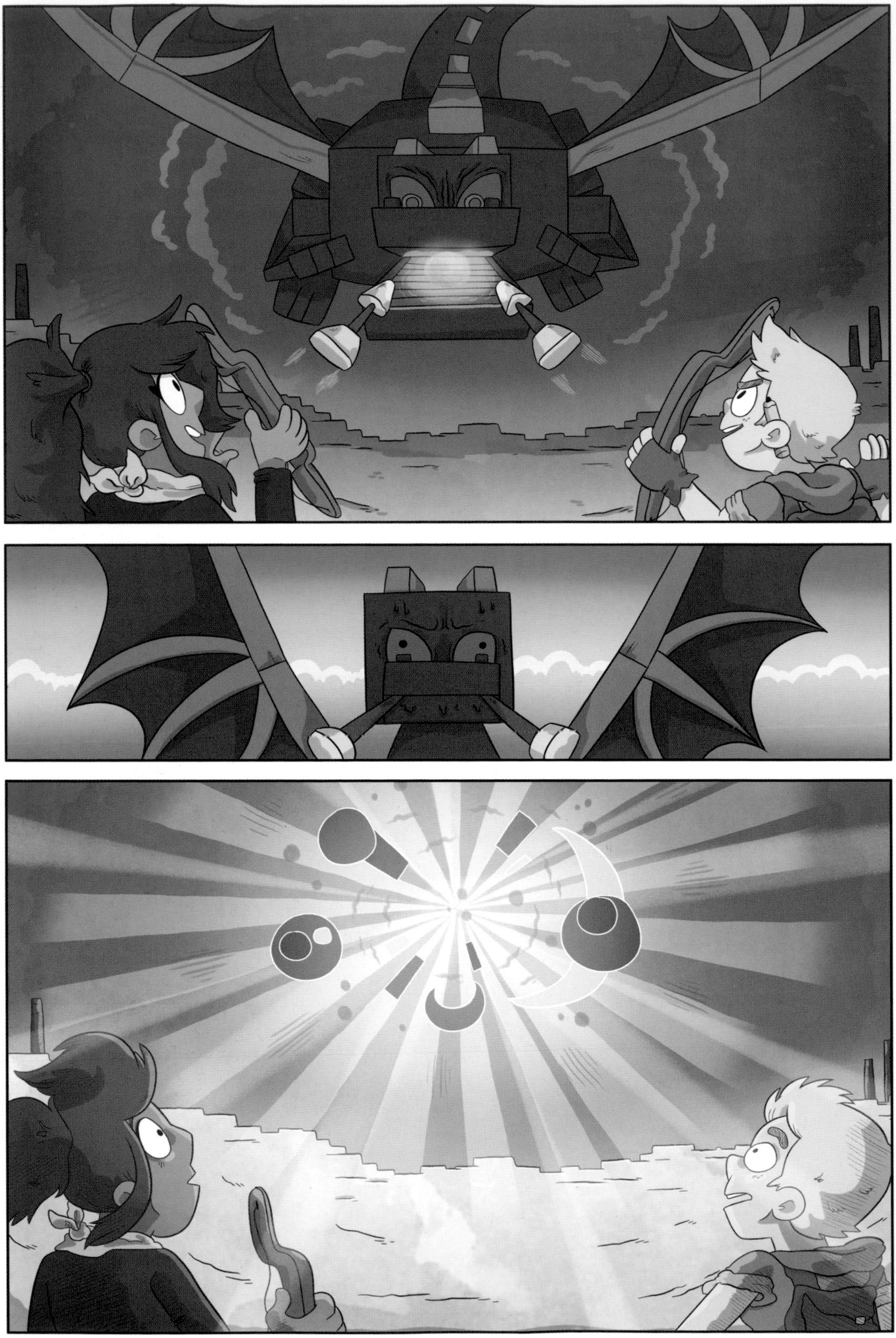

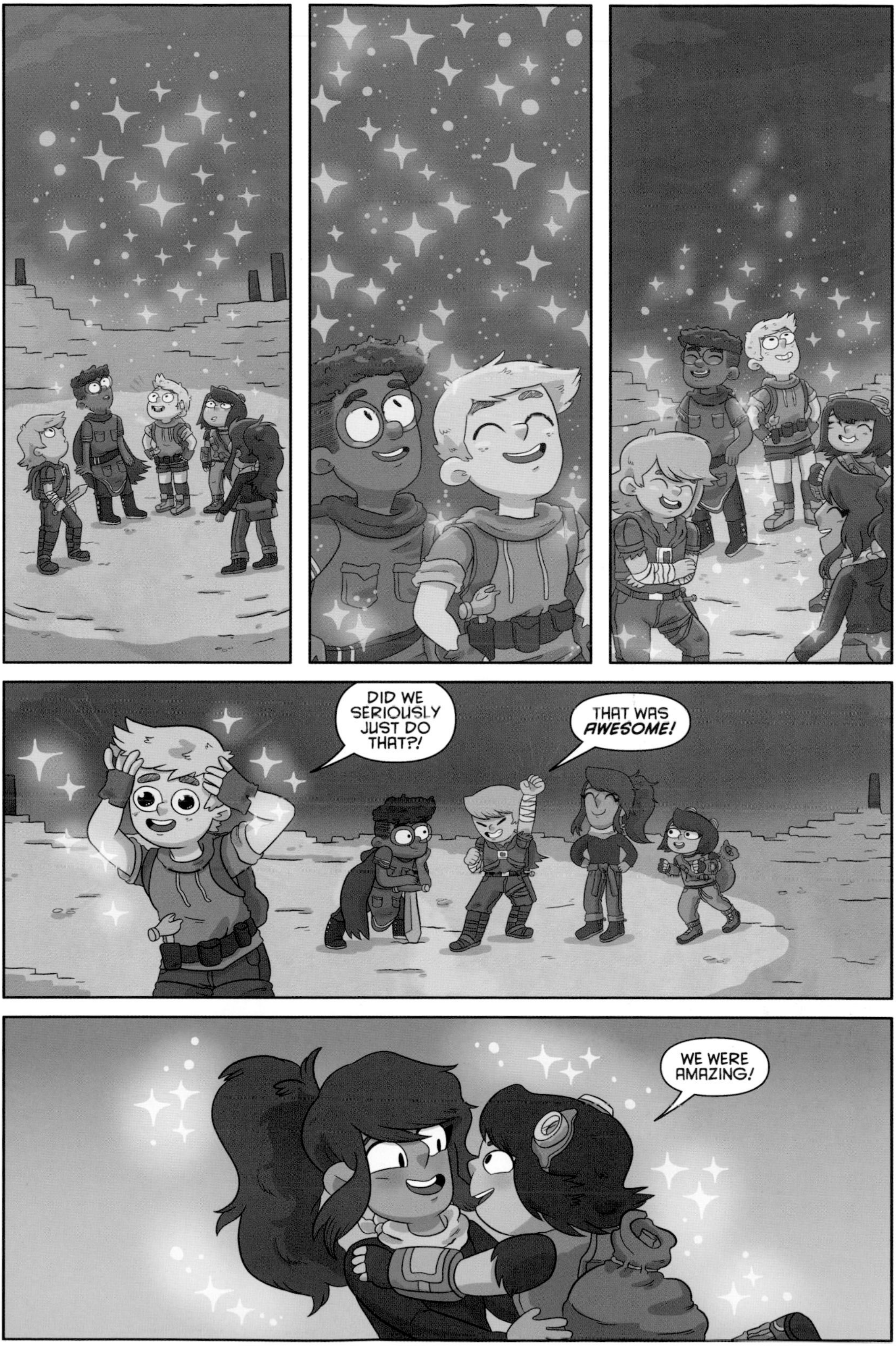
DID WE SERIOUSLY JUST DO THAT?!
THAT WAS *AWESOME!*
WE WERE AMAZING!

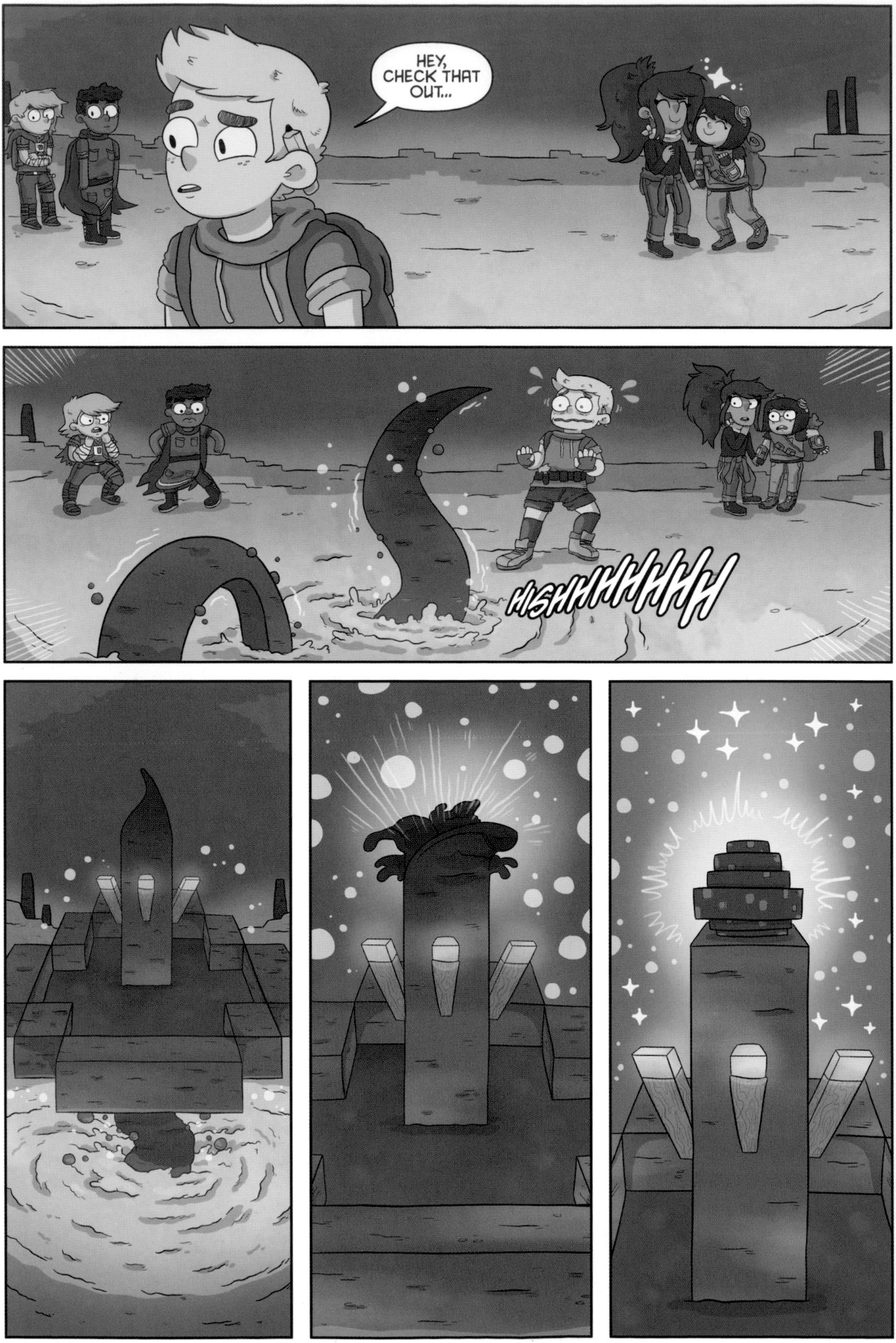
HEY, CHECK THAT OUT...
HISHHHHHHHH

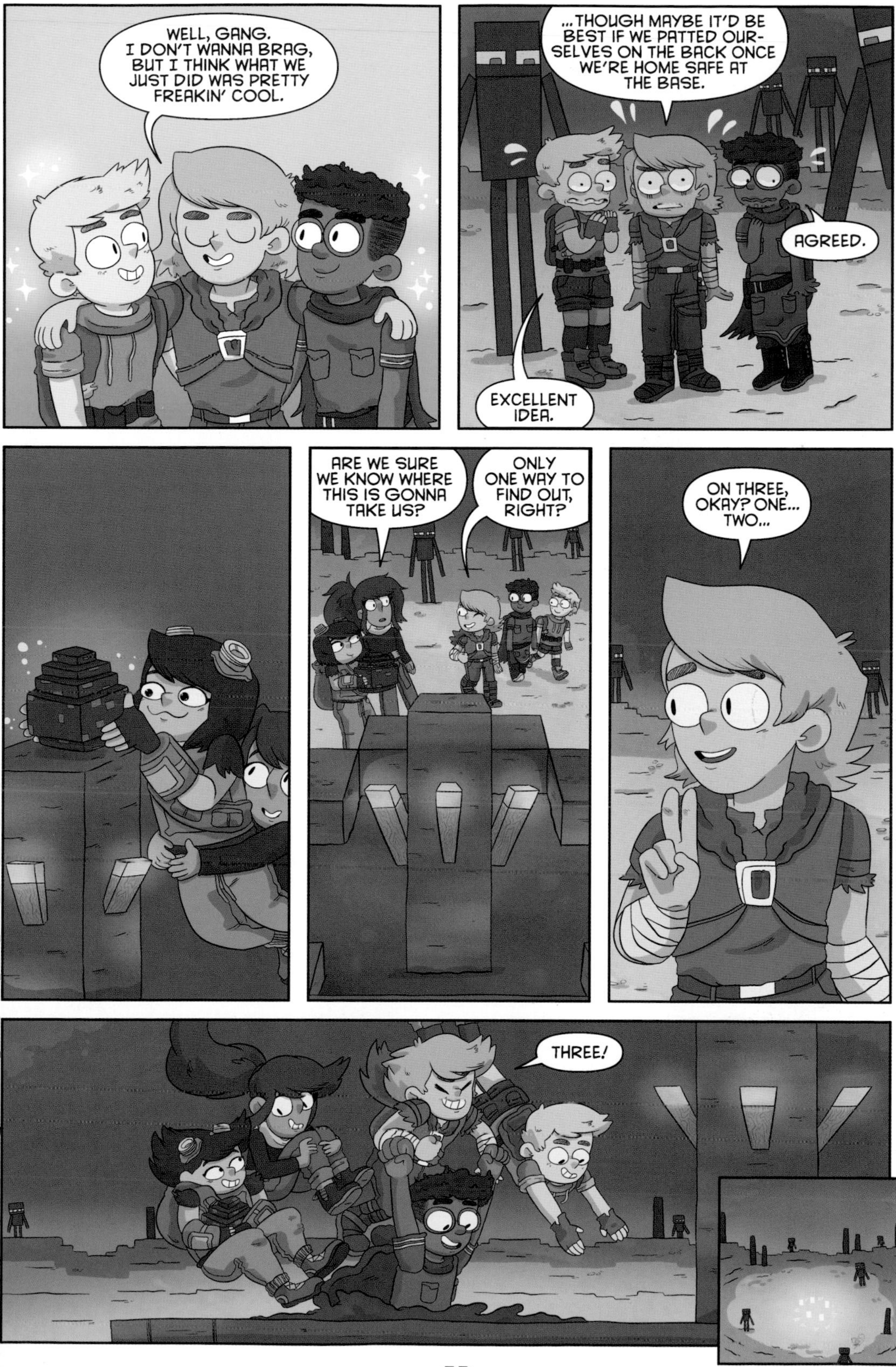
WELL, GANG. I DON'T WANNA BRAG, BUT I THINK WHAT WE JUST DID WAS PRETTY FREAKIN' COOL.
...THOUGH MAYBE IT'D BE BEST IF WE PATTED OUR-SELVES ON THE BACK ONCE WE'RE HOME SAFE AT THE BASE.
AGREED.
EXCELLENT IDEA.
ARE WE SURE WE KNOW WHERE THIS IS GONNA TAKE US?
ONLY ONE WAY TO FIND OUT, RIGHT?
ON THREE, OKAY? ONE... TWO...
THREE!

PAFFFF

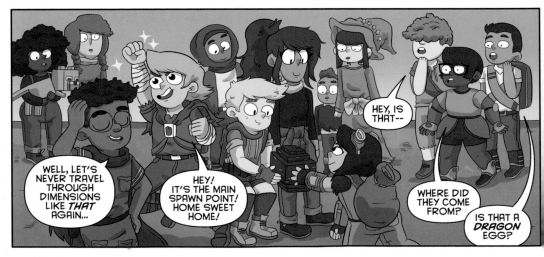

WELL, LET'S NEVER TRAVEL THROUGH DIMENSIONS LIKE *THAT* AGAIN...

HEY! IT'S THE MAIN SPAWN POINT! HOME SWEET HOME!

HEY, IS THAT--

WHERE DID THEY COME FROM?

IS THAT A *DRAGON* EGG?

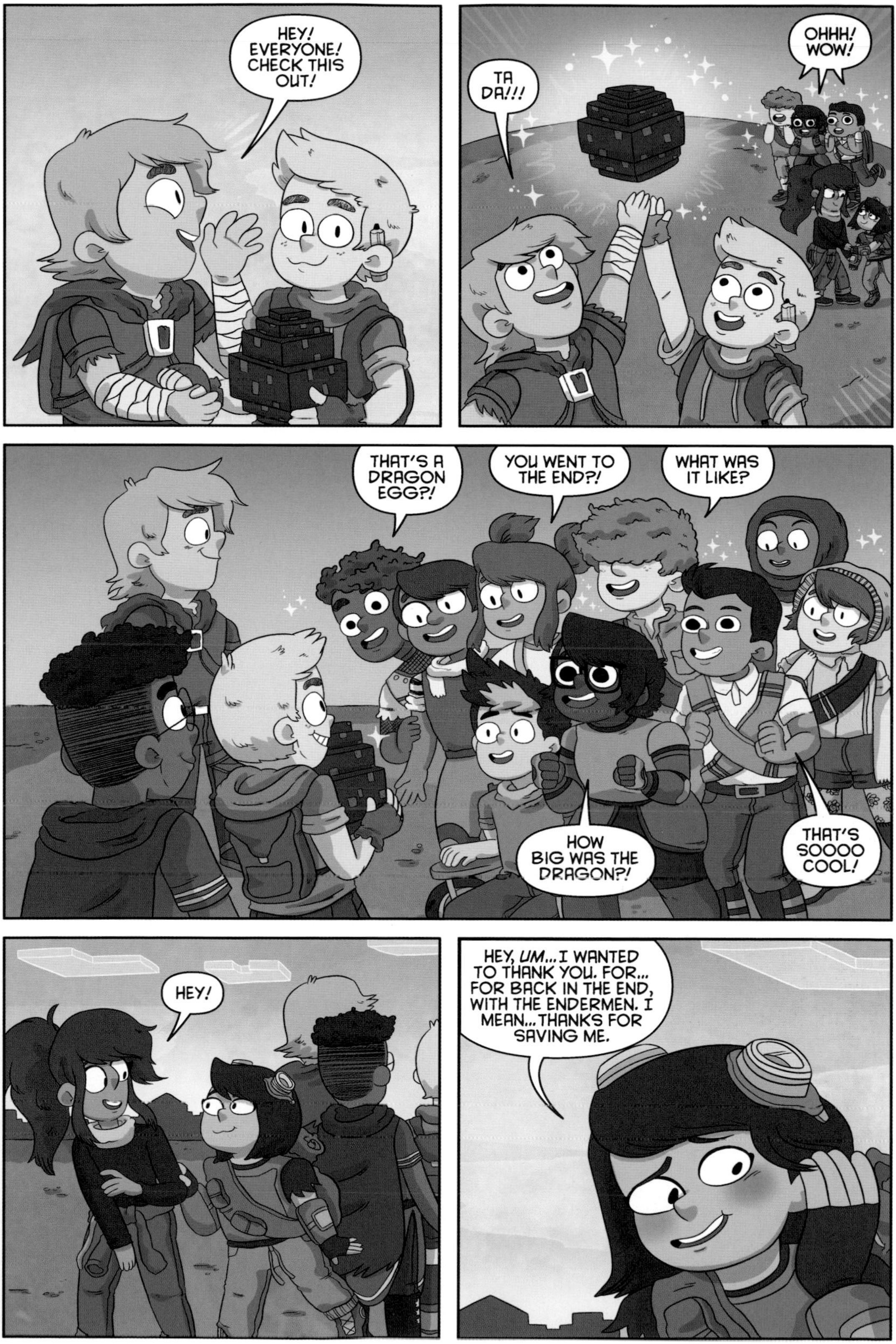
HEY! EVERYONE! CHECK THIS OUT!
TA DA!!!
OHHH! WOW!
THAT'S A DRAGON EGG?!
YOU WENT TO THE END?!
WHAT WAS IT LIKE?
HOW BIG WAS THE DRAGON?!
THAT'S SOOOO COOL!
HEY!
HEY, UM... I WANTED TO THANK YOU. FOR... FOR BACK IN THE END, WITH THE ENDERMEN. I MEAN... THANKS FOR SAVING ME.

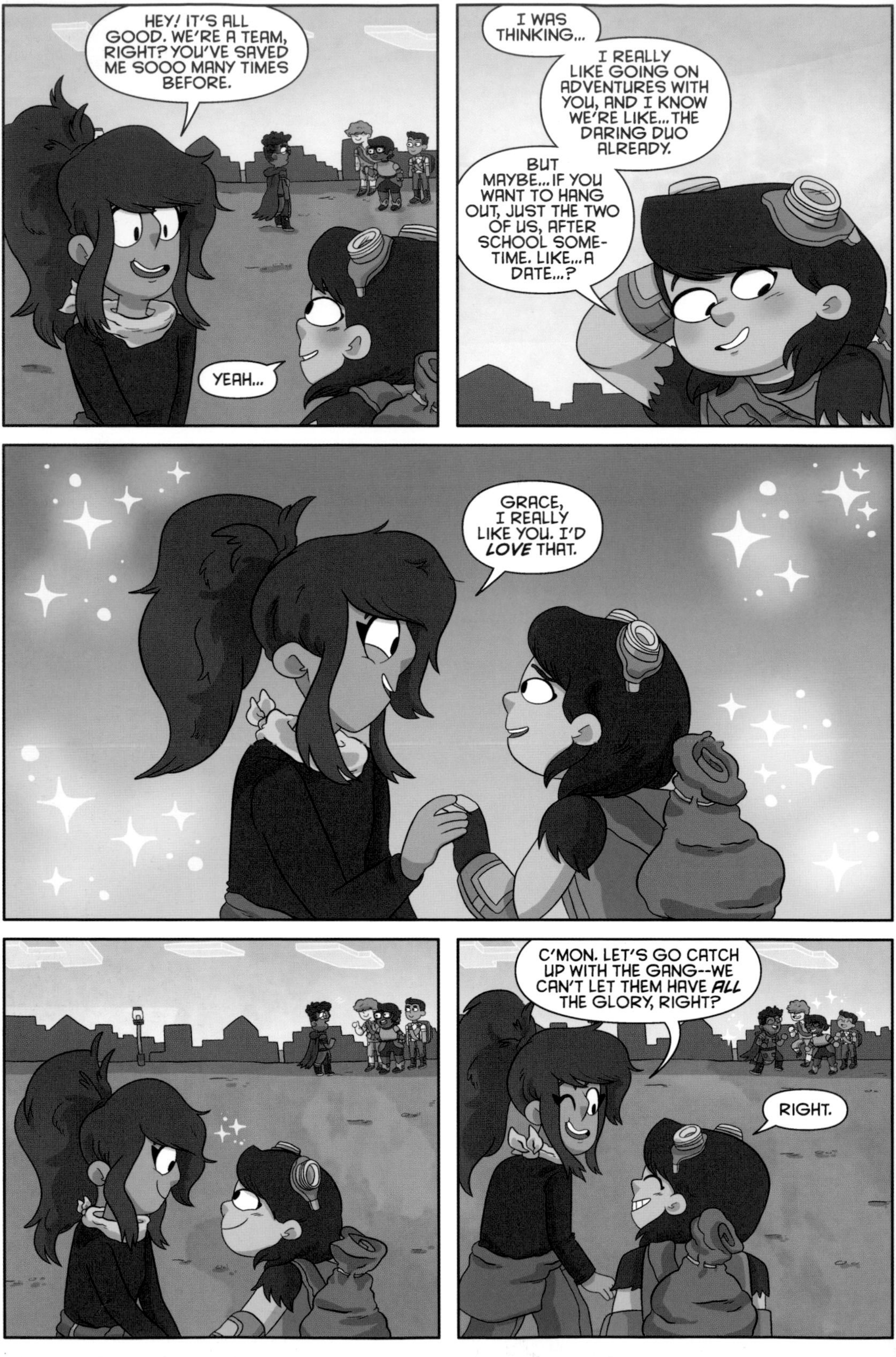
HEY! IT'S ALL GOOD. WE'RE A TEAM, RIGHT? YOU'VE SAVED ME SOOO MANY TIMES BEFORE.
YEAH...
I WAS THINKING...
I REALLY LIKE GOING ON ADVENTURES WITH YOU, AND I KNOW WE'RE LIKE... THE DARING DUO ALREADY.
BUT MAYBE... IF YOU WANT TO HANG OUT, JUST THE TWO OF US, AFTER SCHOOL SOME-TIME. LIKE... A DATE...?
GRACE, I REALLY LIKE YOU. I'D LOVE THAT.
C'MON. LET'S GO CATCH UP WITH THE GANG--WE CAN'T LET THEM HAVE ALL THE GLORY, RIGHT?
RIGHT.

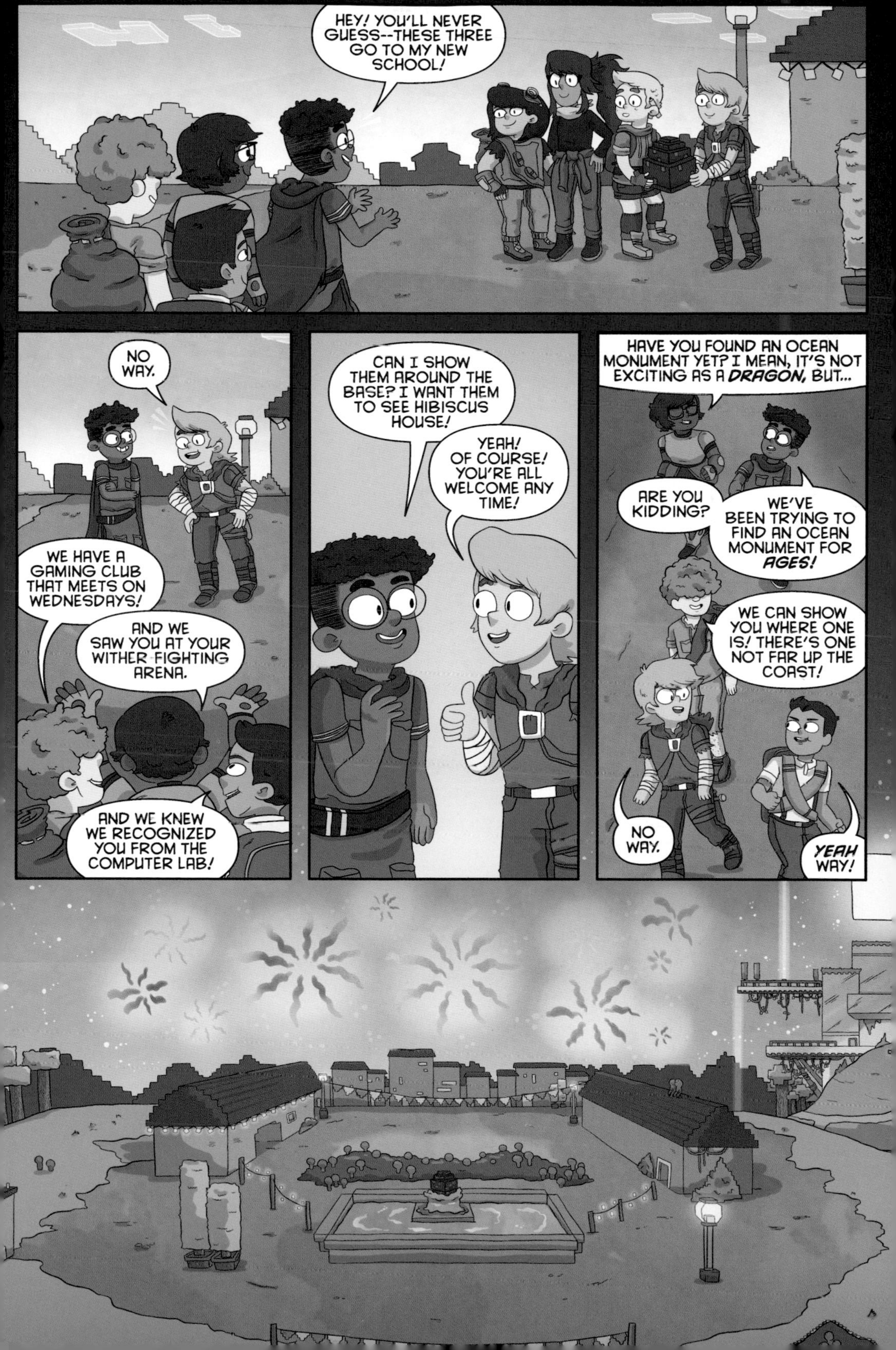
HEY! YOU'LL NEVER GUESS--THESE THREE GO TO MY NEW SCHOOL!
NO WAY.
WE HAVE A GAMING CLUB THAT MEETS ON WEDNESDAYS!
AND WE SAW YOU AT YOUR WITHER-FIGHTING ARENA.
AND WE KNEW WE RECOGNIZED YOU FROM THE COMPUTER LAB!
CAN I SHOW THEM AROUND THE BASE? I WANT THEM TO SEE HIBISCUS HOUSE!
YEAH! OF COURSE! YOU'RE ALL WELCOME ANY TIME!
HAVE YOU FOUND AN OCEAN MONUMENT YET? I MEAN, IT'S NOT EXCITING AS A DRAGON, BUT...
ARE YOU KIDDING?
WE'VE BEEN TRYING TO FIND AN OCEAN MONUMENT FOR AGES!
WE CAN SHOW YOU WHERE ONE IS! THERE'S ONE NOT FAR UP THE COAST!
NO WAY.
YEAH WAY!

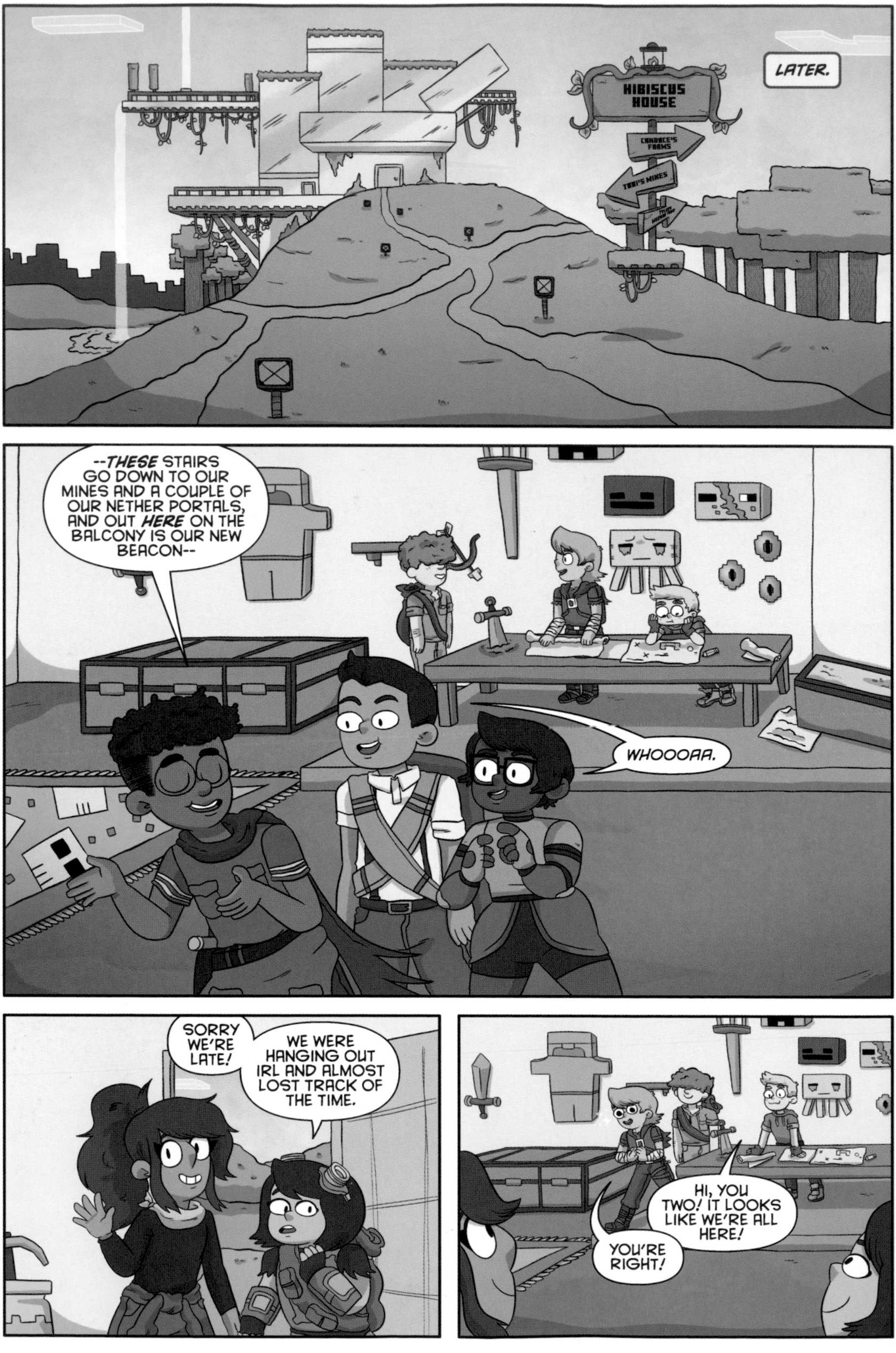
HIBISCUS HOUSE
CANDACE'S FARMS
TOBY'S MINES
LATER.
--THESE STAIRS GO DOWN TO OUR MINES AND A COUPLE OF OUR NETHER PORTALS, AND OUT HERE ON THE BALCONY IS OUR NEW BEACON--
WHOOOAA.
SORRY WE'RE LATE!
WE WERE HANGING OUT IRL AND ALMOST LOST TRACK OF THE TIME.
HI, YOU TWO! IT LOOKS LIKE WE'RE ALL HERE!
YOU'RE RIGHT!

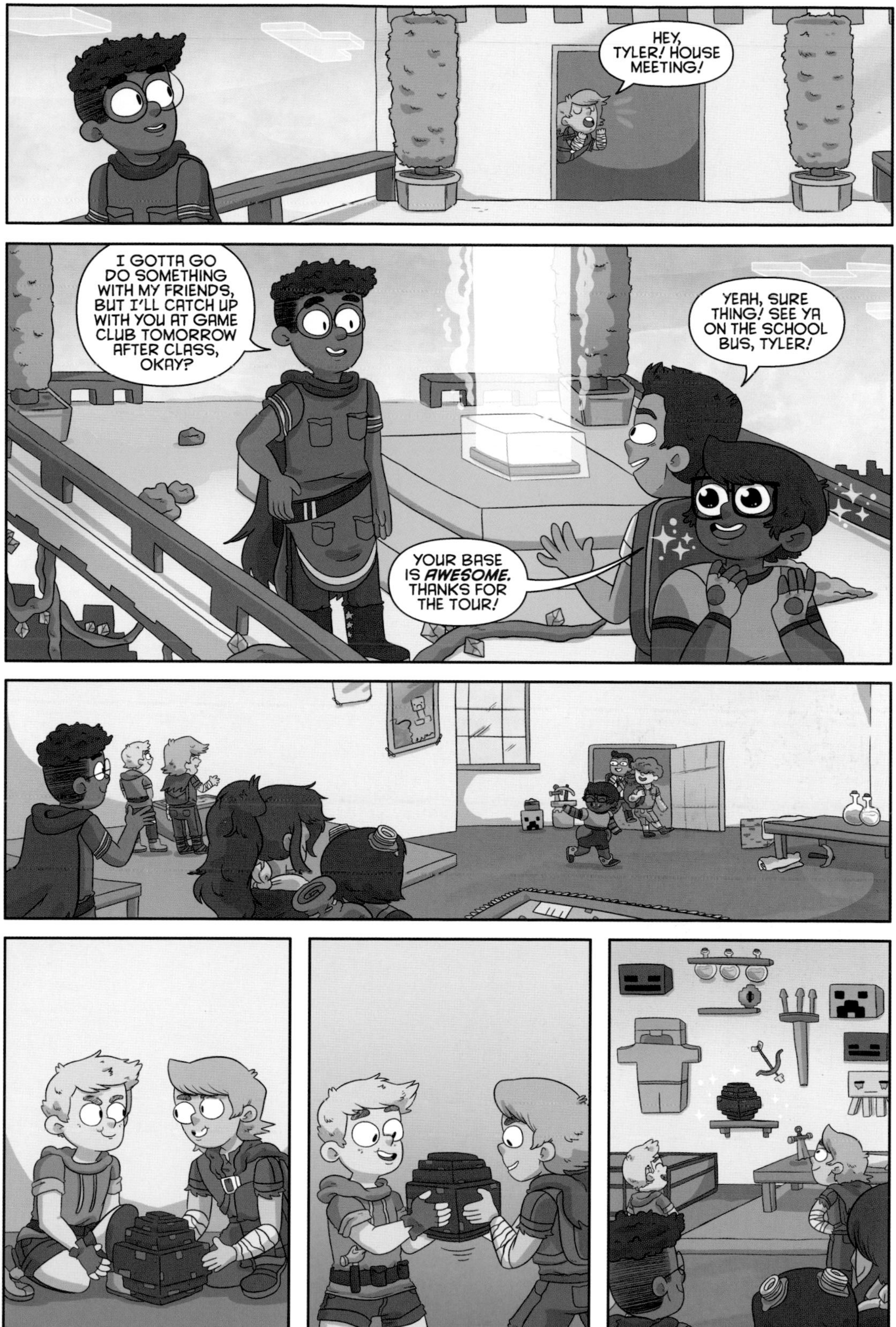
HEY, TYLER! HOUSE MEETING!
I GOTTA GO DO SOMETHING WITH MY FRIENDS, BUT I'LL CATCH UP WITH YOU AT GAME CLUB TOMORROW AFTER CLASS, OKAY?
YEAH, SURE THING! SEE YA ON THE SCHOOL BUS, TYLER!
YOUR BASE IS AWESOME. THANKS FOR THE TOUR!

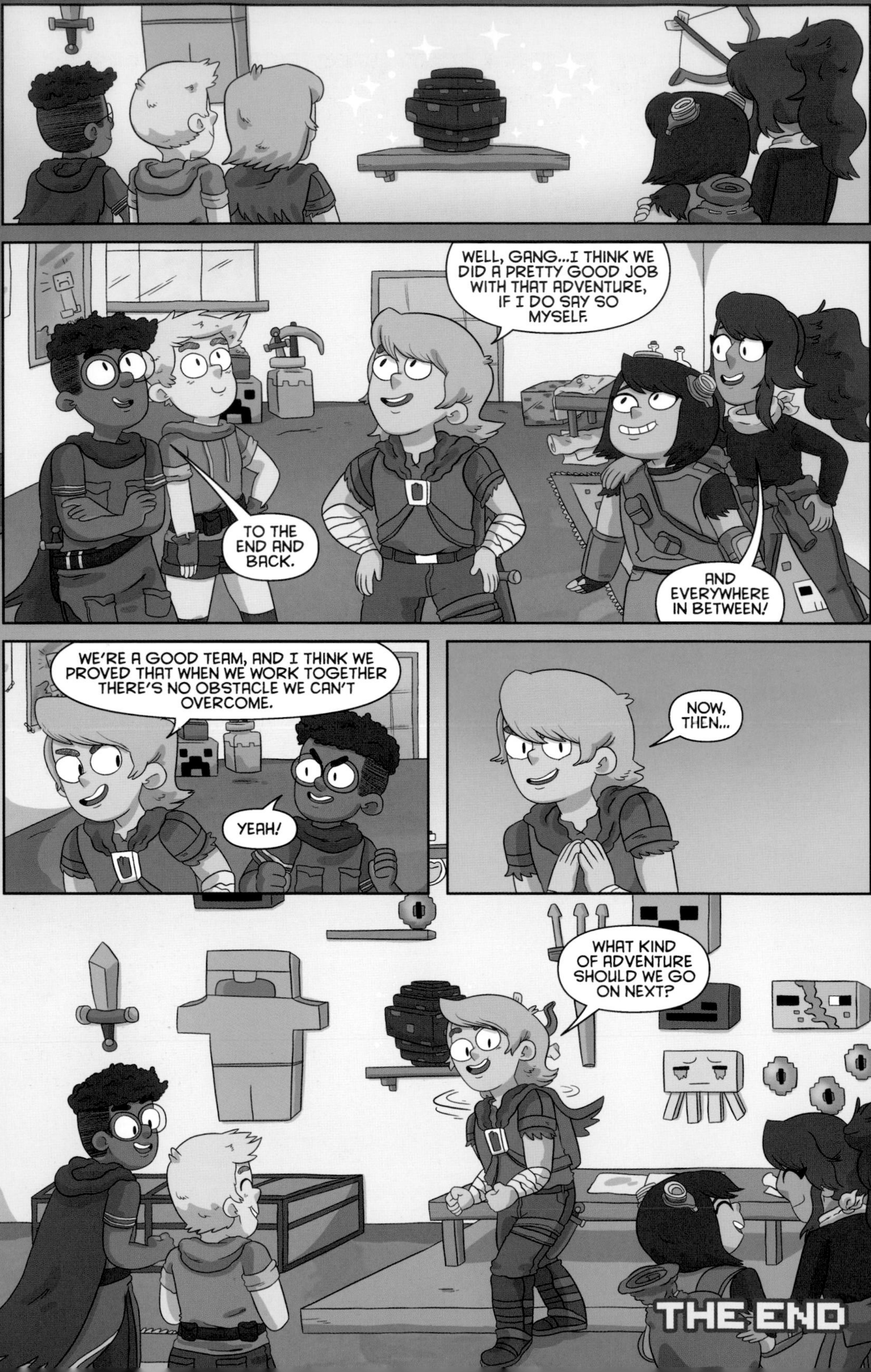
WELL, GANG...I THINK WE DID A PRETTY GOOD JOB WITH THAT ADVENTURE, IF I DO SAY SO MYSELF.
TO THE END AND BACK.
AND EVERYWHERE IN BETWEEN!
WE'RE A GOOD TEAM, AND I THINK WE PROVED THAT WHEN WE WORK TOGETHER THERE'S NO OBSTACLE WE CAN'T OVERCOME.
YEAH!
NOW, THEN...
WHAT KIND OF ADVENTURE SHOULD WE GO ON NEXT?
THE END

MINECRAFT™

SKETCHBOOK

COMMENTARY BY
SARAH GRALEY

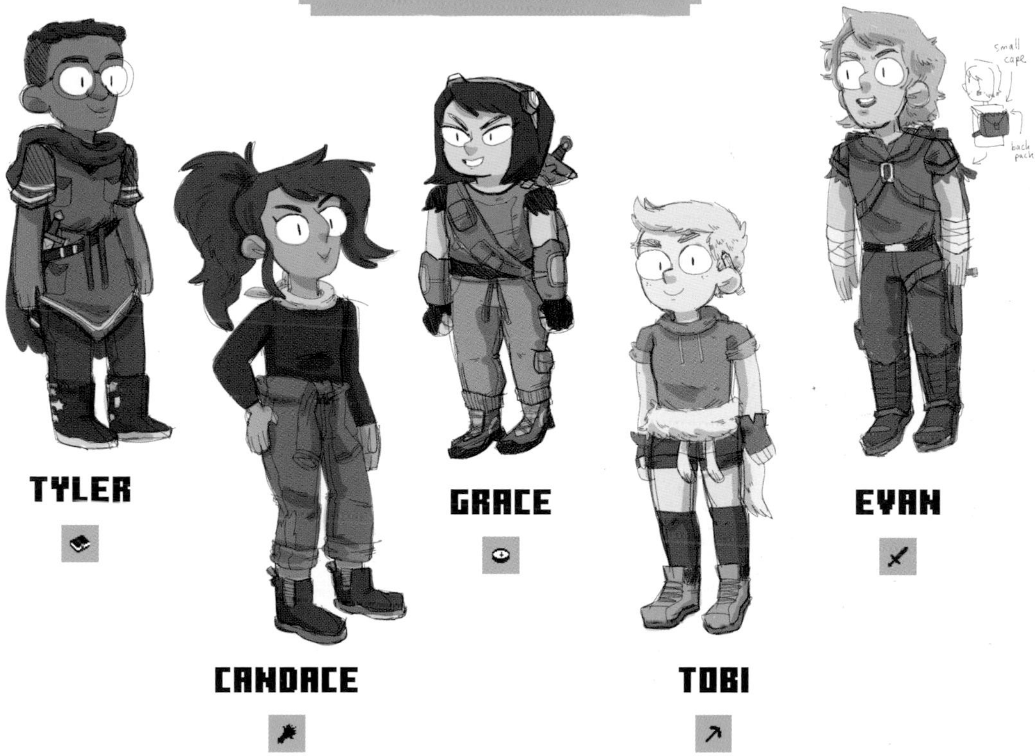
small cape
back pack
TYLER
CANDACE
GRACE
TOBI
EVAN

MAIN CHARACTER DESIGN

Character design is a fun way to express certain traits and elements of a character's personality, and it can give you a good initial idea of what everyone is about! It is definitely one of my favorite parts of the comics creating process.

Sfé gave me some descriptions for everyone—some more detailed than others! Candace was very descriptive whereas Grace was more open to interpretation. As these two characters are my favorite duo in the comic, I really like how the input balanced out between these two, and the collaboration that Sfé and I had designing this wonderful cast of characters!

(Originally Tobi would wear a wolf pelt, but we decided a tool belt reflected their character much better!)

These characters show up at the very start of the book, and then they pop up later in the Minecraft Overworld! This meant that they needed to stand out and be recognizable. They went through a few design changes, but I'm really happy with how this trio of friends turned out!

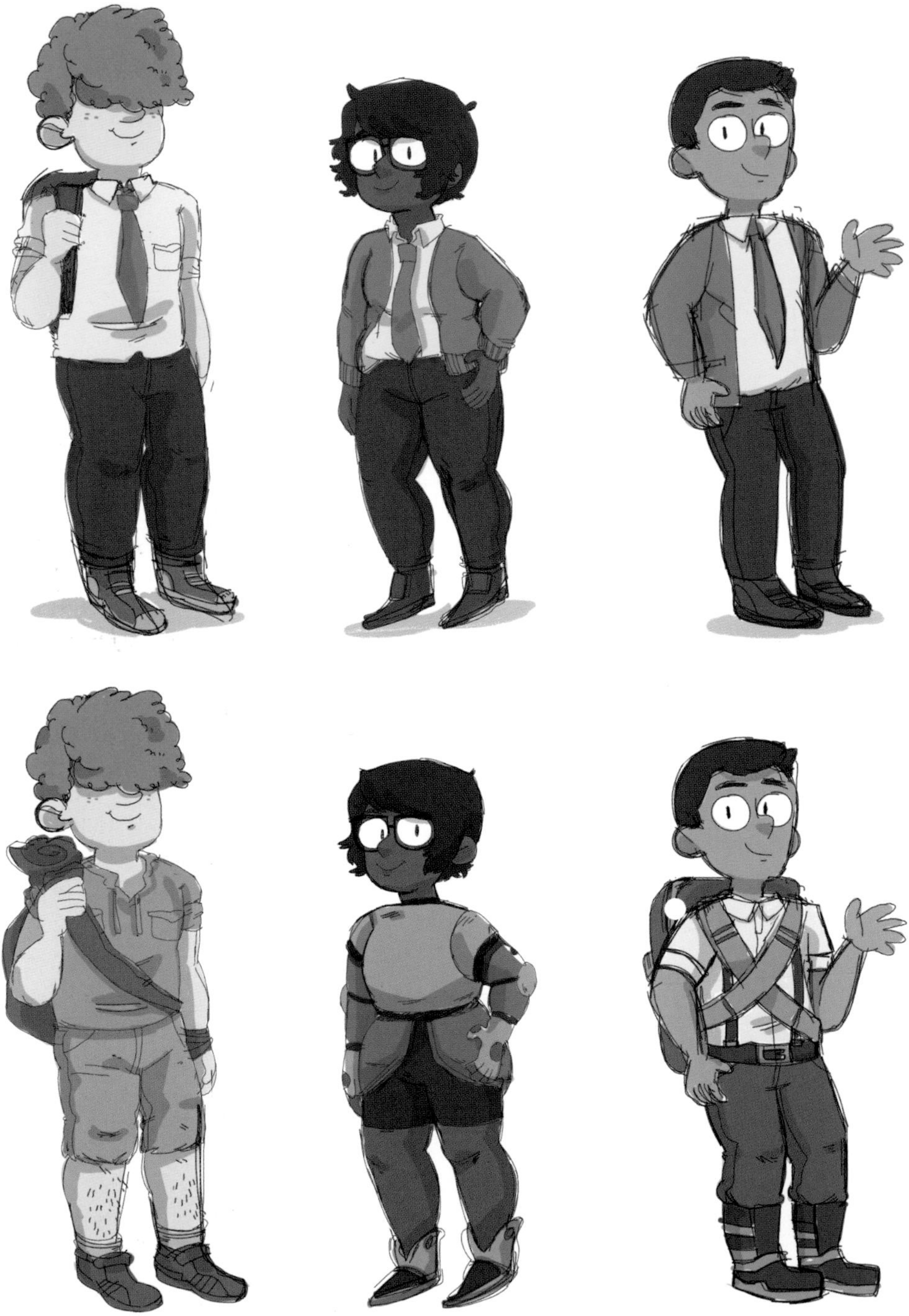

Before starting pencils, I'll usually draw rough layouts for each page of the script. As you can see—these drawings are super scrappy! This step helps me to figure out where all of the panels will go and lets me start thinking about general character expressions before I dive into anything more concrete.

1   **Rough pencil layout**   **2**   **Pencils**   **3**   **Inks**

After the penciling and inking stages, my color assistant Stef steps in—he fills the final inked black and white line art with flat colors before passing it back to me for the final coloring steps!

I then add more detailed coloring work like lighting effects and shading. This is one of my favorite stages, as you can see the final artwork start to really come together!

 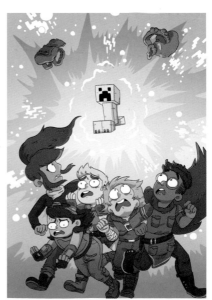

5   **Flat colors**   **6**   **Final colored page**

This was one of my favorite pages to work on! Similar to character design, you can really express and explore a character by what's in their room!

Grace definitely struck me as someone who would listen to a band called CAT MOM, so I just had to give her a cool tour poster for her bedroom wall. It was also really fun showing off the different setups each character was using to play the game!

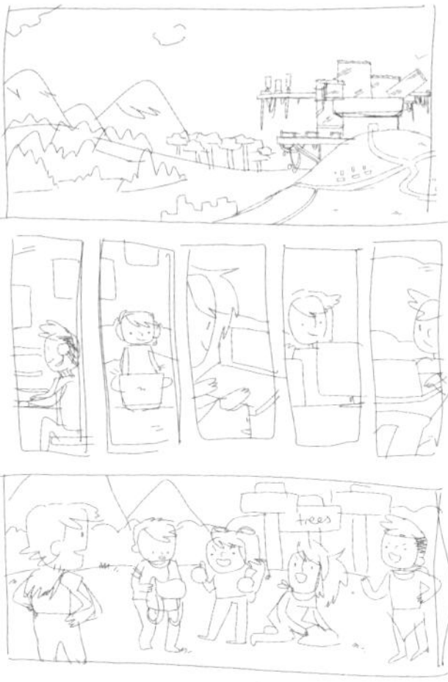

1 Rough pencil layout

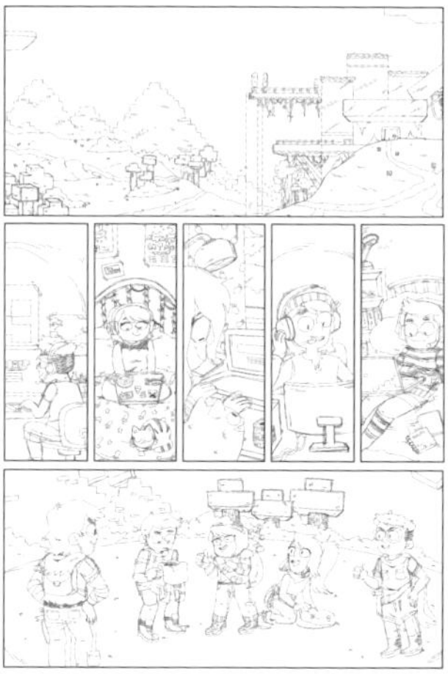

2 Pencils

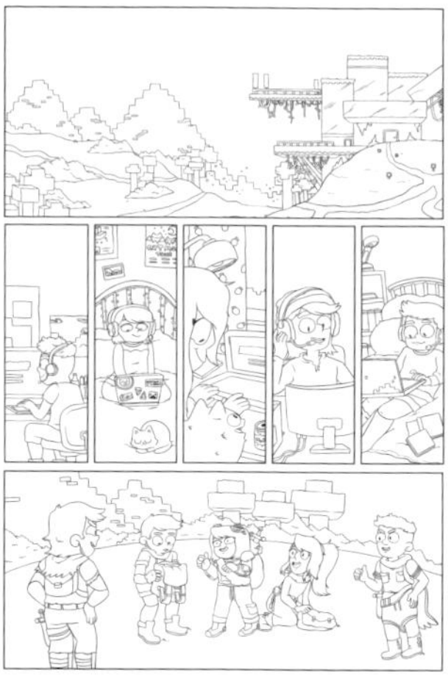

3 Inks

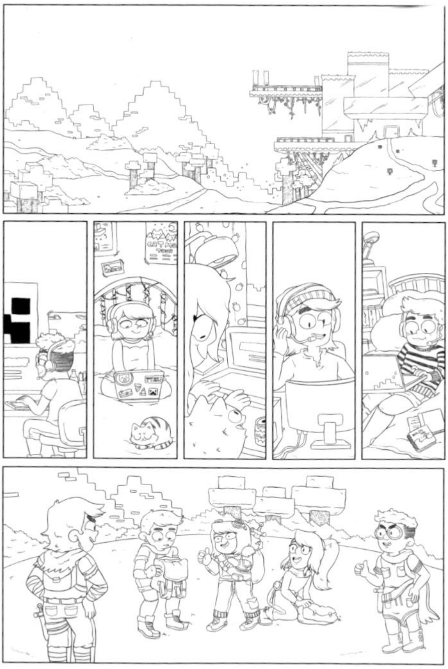

4 Detailed inks

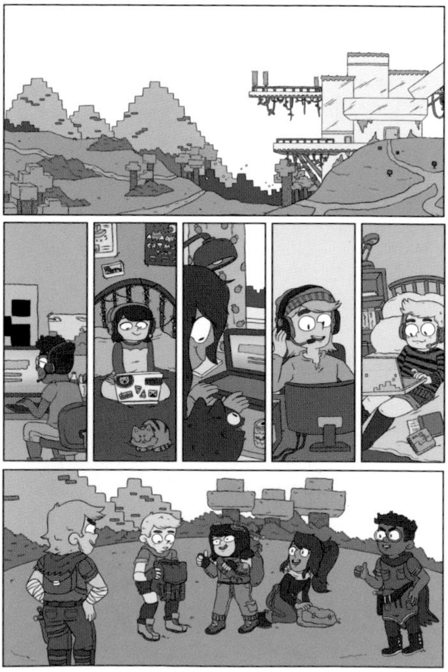

5 Flat colors

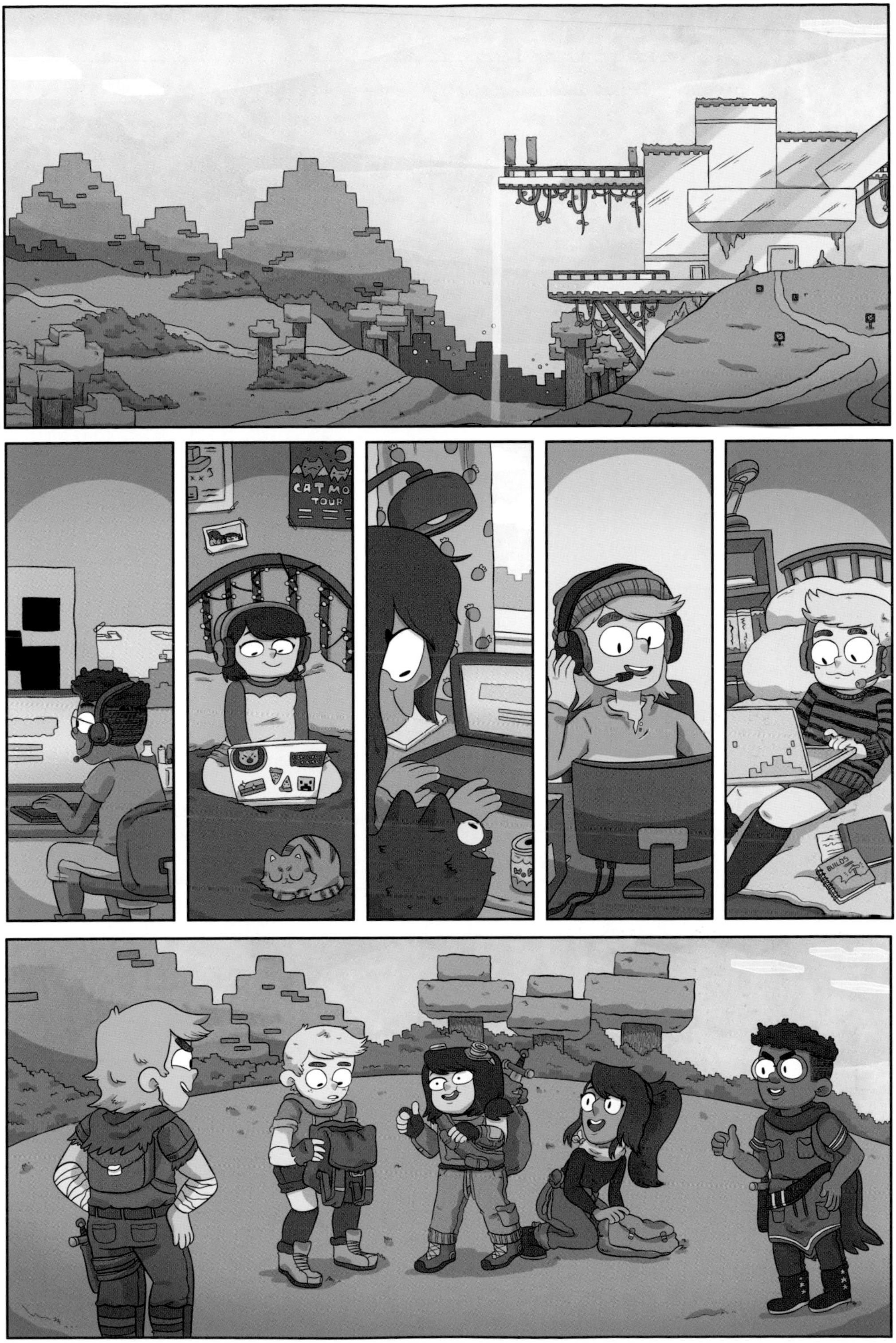
CATMO
TOUR
BUILDS

6 **Final colored page**

For the cover art of the book, I came up with several different ideas to figure out what would represent the book the best!

1   **Rough cover option 1**

2   **Rough cover option 2**

3   **Rough cover option 3**

We went for Option 3, which introduces the characters in a really nice way—Tyler with his potions, Tobi with their construction plans, Candace and her farming, and Grace and Evan with their boundless energy for adventure! It's got a nice blocky vibe and I think it makes you want to get to know these characters and the adventures that they're going to get up to!

4   **Rough cover pencils**

5   **Cover inks**

6   **Cover with flat color**

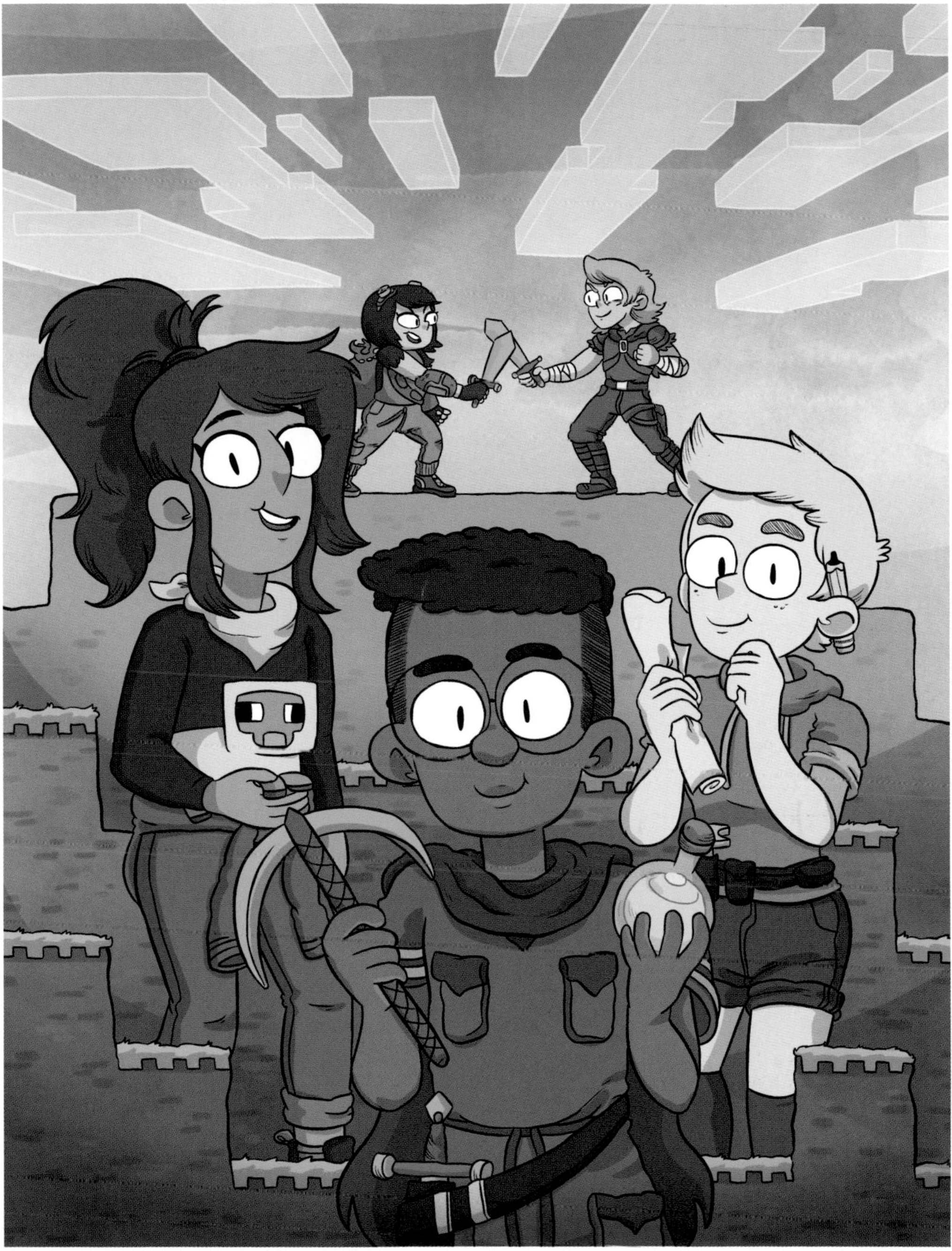

7 **Final colored cover**

The ashcan was a free comic that featured a few pages from the graphic novel as a fun sneak-peek! The preview focused on the construction of the arena, and the wither being summoned!

Options 1 and 3 focused on showing the construction and the wither, while Option 2 was more of a close-up on just the character (and it actually ended up inspiring the main graphic novel cover instead!).

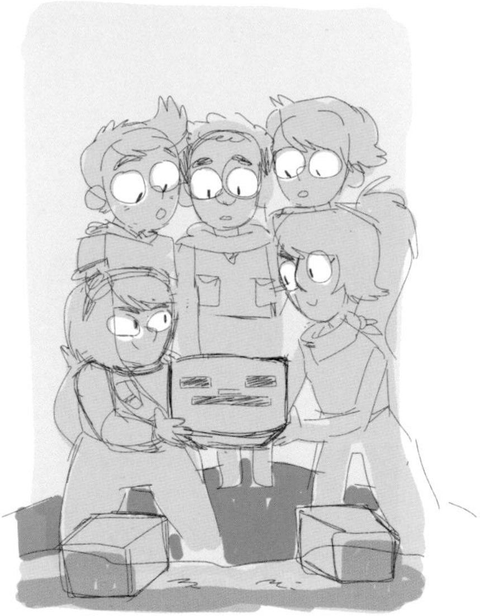

1 Ashcan cover option 1

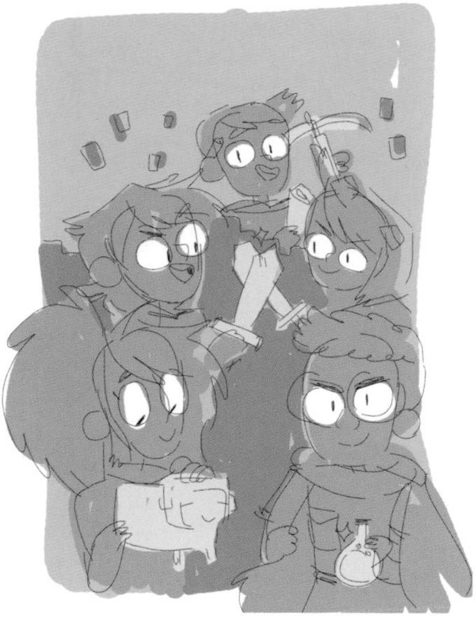

2 Ashcan cover option 2

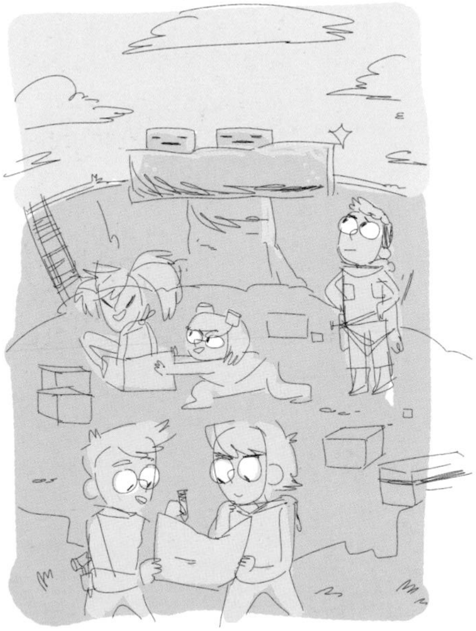

3 Ashcan cover option 3

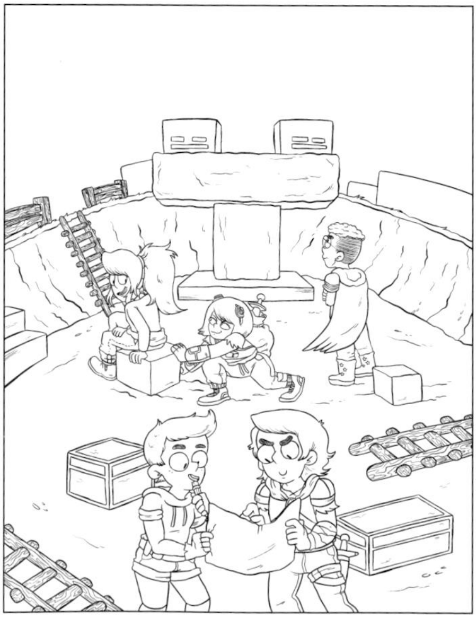

4 Ashcan cover inks

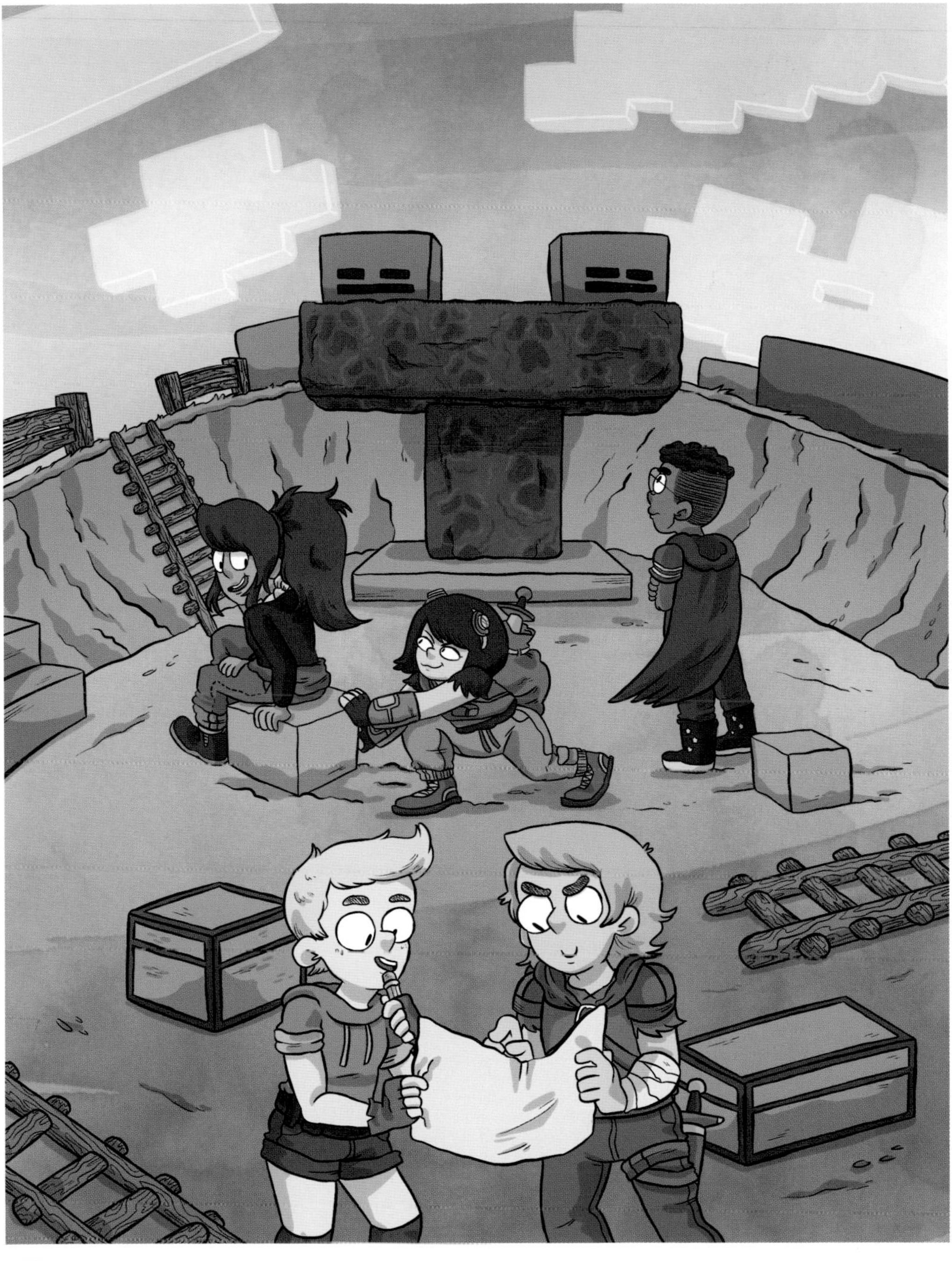

5 Ashcan final colored cover

Option 3 was chosen as the final ashcan cover! It shows the fun of building something with your friends in the Minecraft world, which is one of my favorite parts of the game!

COMING SOON . . .

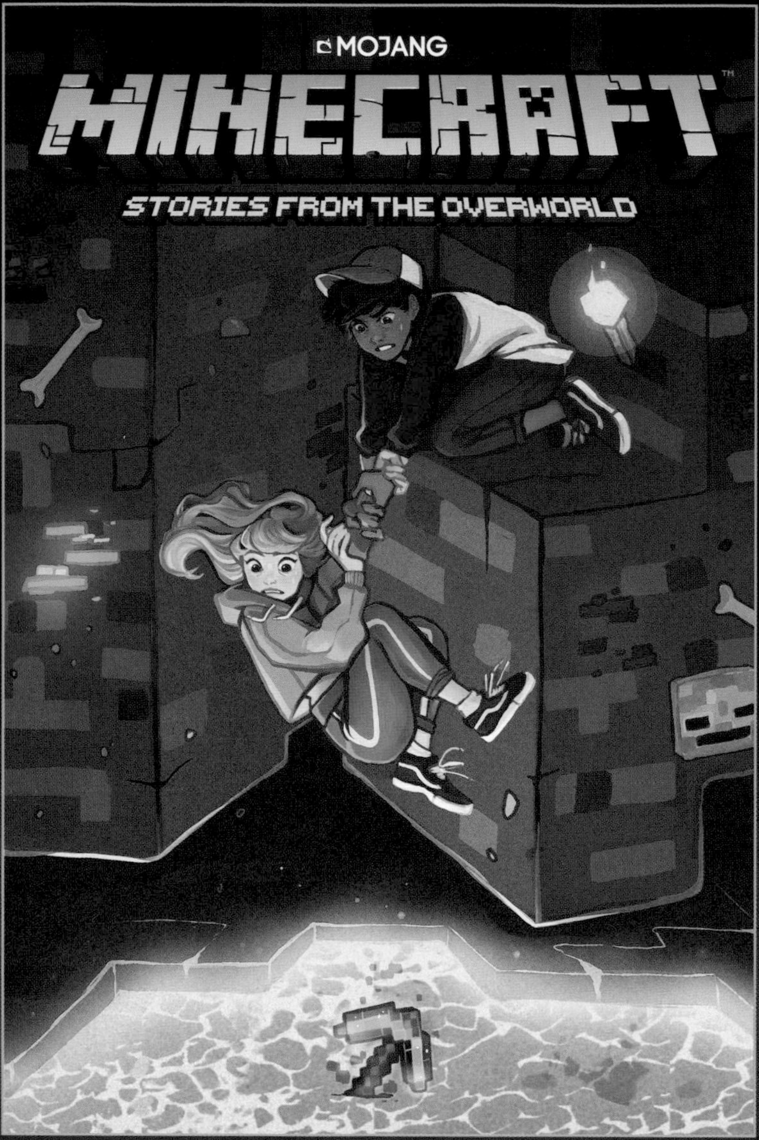
MOJANG
MINECRAFT
STORIES FROM THE OVERWORLD

FROM BLOCKS TO PANELS, MINECRAFT RETURNS TO COMICS IN THIS ANTHOLOGY COLLECTION!

With tales of witch and pillager rivals finding common ground, a heartless griefer who bit off more than they could chew, and valiant heroes new (or not!) to the Overworld, this anthology tells tales that span the world of Minecraft. Featuring stories from star writers and exciting artists, this collection brings together stories from all realms, leaving no block unturned!

AVAILABLE OCTOBER 2019!

Rocket Robinson
and the Secret of the Saint
Sean O'Neill

Stephen McCranie's
SPACE BOY
1

KEVIN PANETTA • PAULINA GANUCHEAU • SARAH STERN
ZODIAC STARFORCE
CRIES OF THE FIRE PRINCE

Bandette
Volume One:
Presto!
By Tobin & Coover

MORE SERIES YOU MIGHT ENJOY!

ROCKET ROBINSON — SEAN O'NEILL

Cairo, 1933—The Egyptian capital is a buzzing hive of treasure-hunters, thrill-seekers, and adventurers, but to 12-year-old Ronald "Rocket" Robinson, it's just another sticker on his well-worn suitcase. The only son of an American diplomat, Rocket travels from city to city with his monkey, Screech, never staying in one place long enough to call it home, but when Rocket finds a strange note written in Egyptian hieroglyphs, he stumbles into an adventure more incredible than anything he's ever dreamt of.

Rocket Robinson and the Pharoh's Fortune	ISBN 978-1-50670-618-4	$14.99
Rocket Robinson and the Secret of the Saint	ISBN 978-1-50670-679-5	$14.99

STEPHEN McCRANIE'S SPACE BOY — STEPHEN McCRANIE

Amy lives on a mining colony out in deep space, but when her dad loses his job the entire family is forced to move back to Earth. Amy says goodbye to her best friend and climbs into a cryotube where she will spend the next thirty years frozen in a state of suspended animation, hurtling in a rocket toward her new home. Her life will never be the same, but all she can think about is how when she gets to Earth, her best friend will have grown up without her.

Volume 1	ISBN 978-1-50670-648-1	$10.99
Volume 2	ISBN 978-1-50670-680-1	$10.99
Volume 3	ISBN 978-1-50670-842-3	$10.99
Volume 4	ISBN 978-1-50670-843-0	$10.99

ZODIAC STARFORCE — KEVIN PANETTA, PAULINA GANUCHEAU

An elite group of teenage girls with magical powers have sworn to protect our planet against dark creatures . . . as long as they can get out of class! Known as the Zodiac Starforce, these high-school girls aren't just combating math tests. They're also battling monsters! But when an evil force infects leader Emma, she must work with her team to save herself and the world from the evil Diana and her mean-girl minions!

Volume 1: By the Power of Astra	ISBN 978-1-61655-913-7	$12.99
Volume 2: Cries of the Fire Prince	ISBN 978-1-50670-310-7	$17.99

BANDETTE — PAUL TOBIN, COLLEEN COOVER

A costumed teen burglar by the *nome d'arte* of Bandette and her group of street urchins find equal fun in both skirting and aiding the law, in Paul Tobin and Colleen Coover's enchanting, Eisner-nominated series! But can even Bandette laugh off the discovery of a criminal plot against her life?

Volume 1: Presto!	ISBN 978-1-61655-279-4	$14.99
Volume 2: Stealers, Keepers!	ISBN 978-1-61655-668-6	$14.99
Volume 3: The House of the Green Mask	ISBN 978-1-50670-219-3	$14.99

DARK HORSE BOOKS

AVAILABLE AT YOUR LOCAL COMICS SHOP OR BOOKSTORE!
To find a comics shop in your area, visit comicshoplocator.com.
For more information or to order direct visit DarkHorse.com or call 1-800-862-0052
Mon.–Fri. 9 a.m. to 5 p.m. Pacific Time. Prices and availability subject to change without notice.